Ferro Family

THE ARRANGEMENT 22

By

H.M. WARD

LAREE BAILEY PRESS

www.HMWard.com

COPYRIGHT

LAREE BAILEY PRESS
First Edition: AUGUST 2016
ISBN: 978-1630351311, 9781630351526 (Paperbacks)
ISBN: 9781630351526 (eBook)

THE ARRANGEMENT 22

CHAPTER 1

A dry run at Miss Black's place seems like a good idea, assuming the whole thing doesn't go to hell. If she's hiding records regarding the source of her income in her home, they'll be locked up tighter than a vault. Part of me understands this is incredibly stupid, but there's no going back. God, I feel sick.

We pile in the van with the two nerds, Mel, Marty and me in the back, Henry scowling from the passenger seat next to Sean. We slowly roll through a suburban neighborhood, passing landscaped houses with solar lights trailing along mulched beds leading to the inviting front doors. Cement walkways shift to stone, as the driveways change from concrete to intricately patterned brick pavers. We're in the upper-class area now. Sean drives up and down the streets, searching for an address and scoping out the neighborhood.

I don't want to be here. Thoughts flutter inside me like drunken bats, bouncing off my brain and landing with a THUD in my stomach. I don't want to do this, but I have no choice. There's no way to hide, no way to erase the past few weeks and pretend they never happened. If I don't do this now, I'm as good as dead. It makes my stomach twist and my throat tighten, but I have no alternatives. Kill or be killed isn't the type of situation I thought could ever happen to me. Not in a million years. I understand why my parents didn't tell me, why they kept their secret—so I could live without fear, ignorantly enjoying my childhood. Had I not discovered how they tried to hide, how they spent years running, constantly watching over their shoulders, only to die anyway, I might have taken that path instead. I might not have chosen to kill someone to protect myself. Murder should never be the first choice, but can be a dark reality when life bends you past your breaking point.

There's a hollowness in Sean's eyes when he doesn't notice I'm watching. He stares blankly, lost in thought, lost in the past. The Ferro mansion is a pile of rubble. He's lucky he only lost his mother—it was possible he could have lost his entire family in that single explosion. I'm glad he doesn't have to endure that pain. For once, I'm glad I didn't grow up with siblings. I can't imagine pulling them into this. Apologizing wouldn't fix a damned thing.

We're going to be lucky to walk away from this alive. I'm not a fool. I know the odds are against us. But when there's nowhere else to go, no other plan of action to free us, we have to stand and fight back.

Marty sits at my side, cautious, perched on the wheel-well, while I sit on the floor with my knees hugged to my chest, head tipped against the side of the van. His dark blonde hair is pushed back, slicked away from his eyes. There's an empty can of gel somewhere. For possibly the first time since we met, I can see his whole face. The angular features of his cheek and jawline, coupled with the worry lines pinching the smooth skin between his brows and at the corners of his eyes, reveal his age to be older than me by several years. When his hair was a mop hanging in his face, he looked younger, innocent.

Marty glances at me as we drive through the darkness toward Black's house. Those warm brown eyes see the things Sean misses. I know he senses I'm going to implode, that there's too much remorse simmering inside of me, filling my mind with poison. It festers, turning my mood rancid.

I have no idea how Marty walks around with blood on his hands, how he can look in the mirror and see anything but a murderer. I've killed. The act of snuffing out another life is not something that vanishes, and it doesn't matter if it was justified. It still stains me in a way that is impossible to treat. A little Stain Stick won't wipe my past clean. Nothing will.

My mind jumps to memories of Amber, but skitters away quickly, not wanting to fixate on her at all. It doesn't matter, though. The center of my chest fills with concrete, and I can barely swallow. There's a trail of bodies in my wake, so many lives lost. Even if it's not my fault, it still feels like it is—it's as if I killed her with my own two hands. Amber lived with me. She has a family somewhere who loved her, and now she's gone.

We roll slowly down another street in Black's Eastern Long Island neighborhood, passing homes nestled on half an acre and surrounded by towering trees. As we roll by, a yellow sign reading, HORSE CROSSING, catches my eye.

Mel sits across from me, her feet tucked under her butt with her hands on her thighs, her eyes burning a hole into the side of my face. She's leaning forward a little, ready to pounce. Her eyebrows knit together, and I can't stand it anymore.

I finally lift my head from the wall of the van and glare at Mel, "What? Why are you staring at me like that?"

Mel cocks her head, making her gold hoop earrings sway. "Stop thinking."

I frown involuntarily, then glance up at her and ask, "Are you telling me you don't think about anything? Like anything? Ever?"

"No," she says, matter-of-factly. "I don't relive things I can't change. I see that look in your eye—you're thinking about something you didn't want to do. It's over, Avery. Focus on what lies ahead."

I avoid her gaze and find myself looking at Sean's profile again. "The past doesn't work like that, Mel. It's always there. It doesn't go away just because I want it to leave."

"If you let it, that weight will settle around your shoulders and crush your neck until your throat closes too tight to breathe. That's when you jump off a bridge or wander onto the Expressway begging God to be hit by a big rig. Fight, Avery. Chase it away. Surviving doesn't mean shit if your brain is too jacked up to enjoy living."

Mel has a somber expression on her face. She's wearing a dark tracksuit with the hood pulled loosely over her head, her gold earrings glinting in the darkness.

I turn away, desperate to look anywhere else. Sean and Henry sit rigid and silent in the front. Goatee and Justin are crammed into a corner, looking paler than usual. Marty stares out a window silently. A chainsaw couldn't cut through the tension in the vehicle.

I squirm and look up at Sean. "Why are we circling her house? We've been down this street four times already."

Henry sighs and glances back over his brown tweed shoulder at me. "We're looking for anomalies, other possible residences she may use in conjunction with her primary home. Like this one," he points as we drive by a small white house. "It's registered to Cecelia Black—that was her mother."

Mel barks, "How'd you know that? I don't even know Black's first name. How'd you find out who her mother was?" Mel glances at me and adds, "I totally thought Black was a fake name."

"Me too," I admit.

Sean lingers at a stop sign and turns, looks at me, and explains, "Henry possesses an exceptional talent for research—especially information buried for years, for which supposedly no records remain."

Henry scoffs, "There's always a record. What idiot would think there wasn't?" He picks a piece of lint off his black sweater vest and watches it fall to his slacks, frowns, and repeats the movement.

Mel offers, "Black? Am I right? I'd bet a Benjamin she thought there wasn't a trace of her past anywhere."

"She wiped everything years ago," Sean says, nodding, "but there's always someone who remembers—some overlooked source who knows the truth."

"And if you find said person," Henry continues shaking the piece of lint off his fingertip, "and offer a financial incentive to recall forgotten things, it's amazing what information you can attain." Speck forgotten, he beams as he glances back at us. His gaze meets Mel's, and he winks at her.

"Big deal," Mel blurts out, frowning. "You waved your money around and discovered her name. So spill, what is it?"

Henry is practically giddy. He grips the back of the seat, pivoting completely around and beaming at us. "You couldn't possibly guess! It's as if the woman wanted to be Rumpelstiltskin!"

Mel isn't amused. Her face is devoid of expression. She says flatly, "What's her name?"

CHAPTER 2

Henry makes an annoyed sound in the back of his throat. "Honestly, you're no fun at all. Her full name is Razelleia Vita Black."

I speak up, "Sean, did you know that?" They had a thing for a while, so he probably knew. I don't ask him much about that relationship. It's in the past, and he's no longer the same man.

Sean shakes his head and glances over his shoulder, his eyes sincere in the amber light from the streetlamp. "No, she never told me."

That's weird. Black talked about Sean like their relationship was close. Maybe the intimacy was one-sided and lived mostly in someone's crazy mind. I prod a bit more. "I thought you were friendly at one point. What did you call her?"

"Babe," Mel snorts, reaches across, and chucks my knee, laughing.

Sean rolls his eyes. "It wasn't like that. We kept things formal. There was no use of first names, and I'd prefer not to speak of this in present company."

I don't answer. Instead, I concentrate on Sean's chiseled profile and the sweep of his dark hair. Although it was a long time ago, it still makes me ache for him. Not in a dirty way, but in a soul-crushing, hideously sad way. Sean wasn't close to anyone for a long time. It must have been awful to go through so much while being that isolated.

"Bloody lunatics, the both of you." Henry spits out the words, suddenly devoid of his trademark light, teasing tone. Anger rolls over him and he visibly prickles. "What do women see in you? How could Amanda choose to live with the likes of you?"

The van is suddenly silent as Sean's jaw locks. His grip on the steering wheel tightens until his knuckles blanch. Mel's jaw gapes with shock, while I sit painfully aware of how hard that hit landed. Still, Sean doesn't reply.

Henry groans and prattles on, "How could you possibly seek warmth or comfort in this man,

Avery? His previous lovers are worse for the wear from being with him. Amanda is lucky she died at his hand, or she'd be in a lunatic asylum like his other victim—I mean lover. It just goes to show—ow!" Henry stops his rant and glares at Mel, who has climbed over the techies to pop him across the back of his head in the passenger seat.

"What the hell gives you the right to shit on other people's misery?" Mel scolds as she swats at his head again. "You had the hots for Amanda, but she picked Sean. Get over it. The man lost his wife! Do you think he doesn't feel?"

Henry swats back. "Of course not! Look at him! He has about as many feelings as a robot!" Mel slaps Henry in the back of the head—hard. He stills and narrows his gaze at her, yelling, "Bloody hell, woman!"

Mel is stepping on the geeks as she tries to take another swing. "You've got eyes, but you don't see jack shit."

"Who's he? I know a Jack Shat, but that's all." Henry teases.

Mel slaps him again. "You think this is funny? You think I haven't figured out what happened between you and Sean yet? Wake up, white boy!" Mel goes to slap the back of his head again, but he dodges, swaying in his seat. Justin finally manages to crawl to the back of the van with the other guy tumbling after.

"There's no way you know," Henry returns.

"Well, I do." Mel glares at him.

Henry laughs lightly holding up a hand like a historian in a lecture hall. "Enlighten us, madam. Pray tell, just what occurred between us?"

Mel grins, glances at me, then Sean, then back at Henry. "You two knew each other, were friends even."

"Anyone could see that—" Henry sighs.

"I'm not finished," Mel snaps. "You two were close until Amanda came running to Sean for help. He didn't steal your girl. In fact, he did everything he could to keep his distance—but you got suspicious and went batshit crazy on them. You ruined your relationship with Amanda, not Sean. Then you carried your shit over into your work and sabotaged him. Amanda caught you and any chance of winning her back vanished. It's your own damned fault you lost her, so stop blaming Sean for your idiotic mistakes. And for the love of Christ, can we just clear the air once and for all?"

Sean shakes his head slightly and hisses at Mel, "Don't—"

I reach for Mel, warning, "Mel, wait—"

Mel swats at me and glares at Sean. "Sean didn't kill Amanda. There was no murderer."

"What are you talking about?" Henry twists in his seat to see Mel.

"Mel, don't—" I try to cover her mouth with my hands, but she shoves me away. Marty leans forward, intrigued. The tech guys press themselves to the van door, looking as if they're ready to bolt.

I manage to wrap my hands around her face, covering her mouth. I hiss at her, "Don't you dare! It's not your secret to tell!"

Henry is more intrigued now. He glances at Sean. His voice takes on a softness I haven't heard before. "What's she talking about?"

Sean tenses. "Nothing. She doesn't know a thing." He glances at me, thinking I told Mel.

I shake my head. "Sean, I didn't tell her a thing."

"Tell her what?" Henry yaps.

Mel licks my hand, and when I don't move, she sinks her teeth into the meaty part of my palm. I shriek. Then, Mel moves fast and pins me down to the van floor. "Amanda killed herself, stupid. So every time you blame Sean, you sound like a fucking moron."

"What?" Henry glares at Sean, demanding an answer. "The papers said you did it. No one even suggested suicide during your trial."

Sean pinches the bridge of his nose and closes his eyes for a moment. "I wanted it that way. If people had known she did it on purpose, that she chose to take our baby's life with her own, they would have been cruel. It would have broken her parents' hearts. It would have devastated anyone who knew her." Sean glances up at Henry, and it becomes clear he never told Henry a thing because he still thought of the guy like a brother.

There's complete silence. The two nerds glance at the ceiling and twiddle their thumbs like they'd love to be anywhere else. Marty's eyebrows lift with shock, but he doesn't utter a word. No one dares to speak. It's as if he cast a massive blanket over us, letting it slowly settle around us.

Henry's face crumples as he strangles his trousers. "You never said—Sean, why?"

Sean is silent, staring straight ahead.

Mel sighs, and answers softly, "Because he cares about you, fool. While you've spent the past decade trying to ruin him, Sean was hiding the truth from you because he knew how much it would hurt you. If that man is your enemy, I need some new friends. Holy fuck—Sean had your back, and you didn't even know."

I'm squashed under Mel, still pinned to the floor. "And how did you find out all this stuff, Melanie?"

She grins. "I got people."

I give her a look. "Is your people a stocky, middle-aged man who works for the—?" Mel stuffs her hands over my mouth to shut me up. I balk and kick at her, accidentally lobbing Justin's nose with my shoe.

"Hey!" Justin pushes me away. "Watch it."

"Chill out, Nerd. It's only a flesh wound." Mel glances at him, shifting her weight to free me. "If you say it, you're in deep shit. Don't even think it."

Sean lets out a long sigh at the front of the van. "Gabe told you."

"Hey!" Melanie turns toward him, shocked. "How'd you know that?"

Sean twists around and shoots her a look. "Now that everyone knows everything— including two petrified members of my tech team—can we please get on with this?"

Henry is pale, all the color having drained from his face. "I had no idea. My God! Sean, what you must have lived through—all for her." He sits there, stunned.

"This isn't open for discussion," Sean states. "We have a job to do, so let's get it done. The mother's house first, then the main house. I'll park around the block." We've been sitting at the stop sign way too long.

Henry is speechless, as Sean rolls forward and then turns the wheel as he eases into a spot by the curb.

After a moment, Henry breathes, "Nothing has shocked me as much as you just did. I don't know you at all, do I?"

Mel smacks Henry in the back of the head again, "No, you dumbass. You don't, and since we're not on Oprah, let's get moving. You two can kiss and make up later. That'd be something worth seeing, am I right?" Mel waggles her eyebrows at the tech guys, Marty, and me, while Sean presses his eyes closed, channeling enough patience not to kill her.

CHAPTER 3

The tech guys ring the doorbell. When no one answers, they walk around back and pull open a panel on the side of the house. They put something on a wire and nod at Sean. Marty heads to the back of the property, watching to make sure we aren't ambushed.

Sean, Henry, Mel and I enter the small, musty-smelling house through a back door. Twin beams of light cut through the darkness as Henry and Sean flip on flashlights at the same time. Something is beeping. Henry rushes off in the direction of the sound, Mel close behind him. I stay with Sean.

"What are we looking for?" I ask, sweeping my eyes around the room. This room has old lady furniture and smells like mothballs.

Sean drags the beam of light across the room and whispers over his shoulder, "Alarm system."

Mel's voice comes from around the corner, her head poking from behind a wall of yellow paint with stuffed birds sitting on branches that stick out of the wall. "Got it. Come this way."

We walk into a small hallway closet that must have been a bathroom at some point. It's now filled with security cameras and a hugeass computer humming quietly against the far wall.

Henry snaps at me. "Come here and place the bead on top of the unit."

I hand him my bracelet, and he removes the bead, placing it on top of the enormous machine, but it doesn't stay put. It rolls back. Henry frowns, glances around for tape, and pinches his hand across his brow when he doesn't find any. "Design flaw. These should have an adhesive."

Sean offers, "We can stop and grab tape before hitting the main house. For now, do this." He grabs a pencil and then places the bead in front of it. It stays put. "You'll have to stay in here to make sure it doesn't slip and fall off."

"Noted. I planned on it anyway." Henry nods and points toward the screen showing the security feed. "Watch."

The image on the screen plays backward, showing us leaving the house in reverse, while the timestamp continues forward. It's surreal.

"It'll look totally normal. We can walk around as we please, but the recording will show only the empty house." Henry sits at the control panel, uses the keyboard to pull up the recorded video of us coming inside and deletes it. "The only proof we were here is now gone." He glances at Sean. "As long as no one comes around, this works fine."

"Do I need to take the bead when I leave?"

Henry nods. "Yes, if at all possible. I only have two prototypes."

"Can't you make another?" Mel asks.

Henry rolls his eyes and gives her a contemptuous expression. "No, I can't just make another. There's not enough time or materials. Plus that little bead cost nearly a hundred grand to produce."

Mel glances at her wrist and grins. "So what you're saying is I should sell it?"

Henry walks over to her, lifts her wrist carefully and presses his finger to the bead. "If you sold it for six figures, you'd be a moron—as you so delicately put it. It's worth millions."

Their eyes meet, and he continues to hold her hand for a moment. Mel shudders and blinks rapidly, before looking away. Damn, that's funny. They had a moment. Mel isn't going to like that.

I smile to myself and ask Sean, "So what now?"

Sean is wearing dark jeans with that sexy black sweater that clings to his chest and hugs his arms. Coupled with his scuffed shit-kickers, he looks like a badass. He pushes his hair back as he looks around the room, letting his eyes rest on me. His expression softens. "Now we dig through her stuff and see what we find."

"I'll rummage through the hard drive and see what pops up." Henry slips into a small chair in front of the computer and starts clicking keys, pulling up files, and rapidly scanning them for information.

Sean wanders out of the room and down the hall. We come across another old lady sitting room, complete with rose-colored furniture and musty stench. Sean motions for us to head upstairs. When we reach the upper landing, he turns and gestures toward a bedroom door. It's locked. He pulls out a small device, pushes it in the keyhole, and presses a button. The telltale sound of the bolt scraping open reaches my ears.

Sean pushes the door slowly and glances inside before freezing in his tracks. He's holding the door half open, half closed, immobilized. Rage flashes in his eyes only to almost immediately dissipate. The anger on his face morphs into something else, something unrecognizable.

"Mother?" he asks. "What are you doing here?"

CHAPTER 4

I step around the door and peer past Sean to
see her. Constance Ferro sits disheveled in a
scorched red robe. Chains encircle her wrists and
ankles, extending to rings bolted into the wall. I
can't process what I'm seeing. She died. Her
funeral came and went. Constance is dead. I saw
her severed arm. I watched Sean try to save her
from the rubble when his home exploded.

I blink, gaping at her. "What the hell?"

Constance isn't herself. She's pale, weak, and
seems equally shocked to see us. "Sean? How did
you find me? How'd you know I was alive?" Her
voice rasps and is no louder than a whisper.

He stares at his mother, speechless.

I walk over to her. "Who did this to you?"

She arches a brow at me as I study the chain trying to find a way to free her. "You're still around? Sean, it's delightful to see your taste in women remains trashy even in the darkest of times." Her tone lacks its usual bravado, but the old Constance is still in there, brewing beneath the surface.

"Avery is my fiancée, and you will speak respectfully," Sean says, his voice monotonous, without a trace of malice or anger.

Constance laughs lightly as if at afternoon tea. "Be serious, Sean. You can't marry her. Do you know who her father is?"

"Yes, I do."

She blanches. "Well, then. I suppose if you want to bring more murderers into the world—"

Sean turns on his heel and leaves the room. His footfalls fade as the shadowed stairwell swallows him whole.

I glare at Constance like she's mental. "Do you want us to leave you here?"

She laughs again like this is some cosmic joke. "You can't free me. These restraints are mortared into the wall, and the key to the lock is with your charming half-brother. Tell me, did you have a reunion? Were there balloons and cake?"

I kneel down and get in her face. "No. In fact, Vic already tried to murder Sean and me. The bastard wants to kill me then do unspeakable things to my dead body. So, no, we're not besties and whatever he did to you—I know he has worse planned. Tell me, Connie, do you want us to leave you here for him? Or do you want to leave?"

Her aging eyes turn glassy, and she swallows hard. I think she's going to say something nice, but, instead, she hisses, "You won't get a dime of Ferro money."

I don't respond to the statement. My brows lift and my arms fold over my chest. "Do you want to die here? It looks like Vic Jr. set everything up flawlessly. He likes to torment people, and, with the world thinking you're dead and buried, he can take his time."

She shakes her head. "You can't take me. He'll know it was you and your true mission here will be ruined. Sean knows what he's doing. Leave me. Come back when you've slaughtered that son of a bitch."

Her request makes my blood run cold. She means it, every word.

"We can't leave you behind—"

"You can and you will." Constance doesn't say another word. She arches a single brow at me, a dismissal, my cue to leave.

I make a strangled sound in the back of my throat and leave the room. I find Sean at the bottom of the staircase, sitting on the last step, his head in his hands.

I place my hand on his back and lean into his shoulder, breathing in his scent. "So that happened."

"She's alive, but I can't save her. If I take her, Vic will know we were here. If I leave her, he'll torture her. How am I supposed to walk away? She's my mother, Avery." Sean looks at me, his blue eyes filled with pain.

"I'm not sure it matters what you do—she refuses to leave. I tried to get her to come. She threw me out." I try not to laugh, but I can't help it. "She's something else, isn't she?"

The corner of Sean's mouth pulls up, and he smiles sadly, shaking his head. "Okay, we finish this."

"You're going to leave her? Sean, I don't have warm, fuzzy feelings for her, but she's your mom. Sean? Sean!" I whisper-yell as he rushes from room to room, not mentioning his mom again. It's disturbing how quickly he accepts this change of events, but he does. With newly found focus, he searches the rooms, carefully lifting papers, and opening drawers, sifting through their contents in the dark. Once in a while he pauses and shines his light on something, and then continues.

I wander into the room with him and rummage through stuff. I find a notebook in a marble nightstand. The front has a list of regular grocery items, but the back has delivery addresses. It's weird.

There's one entry per page:

Carrots—5th Avenue.
Rigatoni—Dix Hills.
Parsley—Upper East Side.

I frown as I look at it.

Sean pads over and stops next to me, peering down over my shoulder. He's close enough for his scent to fill my head. I wish I could wrap my arms around him and never let go. I show him the book.

"Either she's nuts, or this is a code."

Sean flips through the pages and nods. He takes it, snaps pictures of each page and tells me, "Put it back."

I do as he says, and when I place the book in the drawer, I pick up a brass letter opener. No one deserves to be left alone and defenseless with Vic Jr. I tuck it into my pocket and continue searching Black's stuff. When we finish exploring the upstairs rooms, Sean passes by his mother's room and closes the door. They don't speak.

It bothers me. "You're not even going to try to get her out?"

"Avery, she won't come." He stops and looks at me, those blue eyes pleading with me not to make a big deal out of this. "The best way to help her is to finish this and come back for her."

"But what if he moves her? What if he hurts her?"

Sean takes hold of my shoulders. "He already has. There was a body at the mansion. It wasn't Mother, so someone else is dead. If we free her, he'll know we're coming for him. I can't risk it, Avery. If I have to choose who to save, Mother or you, I have no doubts—none." His hands are on my shoulders, and he forces me to look him in the face.

"Sean—"

"Avery, I choose you." His hands linger for a moment, and there's an all-consuming sadness in his eyes that breaks my heart. He blinks, and it's gone. The scary man dressed in solid black is back. His eyes darken, and he turns from me, disappearing down the stairs.

I swallow hard and glance at her door, now locked again. I pull the letter opener from my pocket and pad toward the room before I kneel at the base of the door. I shove the metal object through the crack near the floor and hear it slide halfway across the room before coming to a sudden stop. At least now she can inflict some damage of her own.

Constance's voice comes through the door. "You still won't get a penny."

CHAPTER 5

We're out and back in the van before anyone comes home. Sean's motorcycle is parked in a luxury storage unit a few blocks away. It looks more like an airplane hanger than a personal garage. He stops, enters a key code, and then rolls us into a hugeass concrete room with climate control. Sean slips out of the van and turns the lights on. As they flicker to life, I realize we're in a room the size of a football field and filled wall-to-wall with expensive vehicles—including a biplane, motorcycles, and race cars.

We follow Sean out and everyone gapes, shocked. Henry drifts from the cars, toward the bikes, hands outstretched in a gimme pose, his eyes wide. "A 1958 Ariel Cyclone," he gasps. "It's beautiful. Perfect." His gaze drifts further, and he wanders over, staring as he swallows hard. "Is that a 1907 Harley-Davidson strap tank?" He's practically drooling as he straightens, twists at the waist, and looks Sean full in the face. Pointing, he says, "I tried to buy this motorbike at auction. I offered $700,000 for it, but someone outbid me."

Sean grins. "You should have gone a bit higher. $715,000 was the magic number."

Henry makes a high-pitched giddy noise and asks to pet the bike. Mel and I stare at each other like they're both mental—until she sees a cherry red sports car near the back of the hanger. "Holy shit! Is that a Bugatti?"

Sean smirks and stuffs his hands in his pockets. "Yeah, the Veyron."

She squeals "Holy shit!" and skips off toward it to plaster her face to the car window. She yells back to us. "Why didn't you tell anyone you had all this stuff?"

Sean shrugs. "The same reason I don't walk around talking about the Island. I don't tell everyone everything I own. It's not a good way to win people over."

Henry rounds on him, alarmed, pelting him with questions. "Which island? Where? I bet mine is bigger."

Mel chuckles as she saunters back over, half skipping. "Rich guy problems. My island is bigger than yours," she mimics in a singsong voice. "Ha! Who wants an ugly, old-ass motorcycle they can't even ride?"

I smile and turn, noticing Justin and Geek Boy both wondering if they can touch a bike with the American flag painted on the gas tank, long handlebars, and sparkling chrome. They look up and ask Sean, "Is this real?"

Sean nods and tucks his hands under his arms, smiling shyly. "Yes, I like old movies, and that's an iconic American piece."

Sean is in his element for the moment, all worries forgotten. It's sweet and shows a side of him I've never seen. It sounds stupid, but aside from the few times he's flashed a wad of cash, I forget he's rich. He rarely flaunts his wealth, and I'm pretty sure the sweater he's wearing is from Land's End or the GAP. I'd never have suspected Sean owned a priceless collection of vehicles because he doesn't act like a condescending prick.

Speaking of condescending pricks, Henry slaps Sean on the shoulder and stands next to him. "I had no idea you were the one who snatched that from me. I'd love to take the time to truly examine the piece later—if you'd like to show it off."

It's an olive branch, a peace offering. Sean could tell Henry to fuck off, but he doesn't. He simply nods. "Any time."

Sean hands Marty the keys to the bike he was riding the day we met. Marty jumps on the bike, kick-starts it, and agrees to buy tape from the store before meeting us at Black's. Marty revs the engine, letting it echo in the cavernous room, before pulling out to disappear into the night.

CHAPTER 6

When we climb back into the van, everyone settles in. There's a little more space without Marty next to me, so I kick out my legs. Justin hangs out with Geeky Guy just behind Henry's seat. Mel is sitting across from me, mirroring my pose and looking like she's imagining driving that Bugatti.

Sean steers us back toward the neighborhood we were in before, slowly meandering through the streets, killing time until Marty finds us.

There's still a lot of excited chatter about the collection when he interrupts, "I need to say something. It could change things, so you need to know. My mother, Constance, was being held at Black's mother's house."

"The residence we just left?" Justin's voice betrays his shock.

"Yes," Sean replies darkly.

Mel blanches, "What? Your mother was there? She's dead!"

"I thought she was deceased as well," Sean says, matter-of-factly, his hands never faltering as he continues to guide us toward Black's house. "Apparently, the body at the mansion wasn't her."

I remember the arm, the ring on that slender female finger. I'm sitting in the back across from Mel again. "Why would your mother's ring be on another woman's hand?"

Sean sighs, rubbing his face one-handed while turning the steering wheel with the other. When we round the corner, he confesses, "She was Mother's lover."

Everyone makes a sound of disbelief, questions erupting from every mouth but mine. They all talk at once, shouting over each other.

Sean silences the van with one stern look in the rear-view mirror. "I don't know how long or why she didn't say anything publicly. Ask her yourself when all this shit is over."

I blink rapidly, wondering how Sean holds it together so well. If she were my mom, I couldn't have left her there. I couldn't have walked away. I glance out the window and see Marty streak by on Sean's motorcycle. He waves at us, unaware of our conversation, unaware Constance Ferro is alive.

The world thinks she perished in the explosion. Her funeral was televised uninterrupted, and throngs of mourners placed flowers at the foot of the Ferro mausoleum. Eventually, the front doors became inaccessible, and anyone trying to get near it had to wade through the waist-deep flowers surrounding Constance's grave. She might be a nasty piece of work, but the public doesn't feel that way. They mourned her like a lost princess. It was fascinating in a surreal way.

When we pull up at Black's, we repeat our process from before. The tech guys ring the bell. When there's no answer, they dart around the side of the house and tamper with a wire. Apparently, that's the phone line. The device they clip on it contains a computer chip designed to reroute any calls to Justin's cell number in case the alarm system dials out for help. He can then pretend to be whatever we need. That chip on the line is a failsafe.

When we enter, I glance around. Black's house is modern and sleek. Everything is glass and chrome, in stark contrasting shades of gray. There are a few fine pieces—an antique chaise lounge, a French writing desk, but nothing expensive enough to betray her reported income. On the surface, this is the home of an upper-middle-class woman living alone.

Sean waves me down a long, mirror-lined hallway and into the master bedroom. He rushes me into the closet where Mel is placing her bead on a computer and taping it in place. The monitor flickers for a second as she deposits the bead on the machine.

Henry locates the footage of us entering and deletes it. "Have at it," he says, without looking up. "Only ten minutes this time. Longer than that is pressing our luck."

I head out with Mel and Sean. Marty is canvassing the perimeter, watching for Black and her security detail to come home. If she arrives, he'll tell Henry, who will then tell us, and we'll bolt. I still don't like this—wandering through her house feels like an invitation to get shot.

Mel disappears into one room and Sean into another. I take the last door at the end of the hall. When I open the door into the room, I wish I hadn't. It's a retrofitted gym with dark wood floors, thick mats, and chrome poles with leather tethers dangling from the top. Mounted to a wall is something that looks like it belongs in a torture chamber. It has straps and clamps attached to it directly, and an assortment of removable metal spikes waiting on a nearby table. I cringe. Was

Sean into this with her? Has he been here? In this very room? Did Black introduce him to all this dark, painful sex play stuff? I don't know.

Ignoring as much as possible of the contraptions surrounding me, I head toward the back of the room to a small bed and nightstand. Nervous, I pull the glass knob too forcefully and accidentally pull the entire drawer from its frame. It clatters to the floor, spilling its contents. A bottle of lube rolls to a stop at my feet. I swear under my breath as I shove it back in the drawer along with condoms and permanent markers. As I stretch to slide the drawer back into its tracks, I notice something odd. The inside of the drawer is shallow, but the outside of the drawer is deep. I put it on the floor and push at the corners of the inside of the drawer. It tilts.

"False bottom," I mutter to myself and remove all the items from the top part of the drawer.

Then I push again and grab a corner as it lifts. Beneath the board rests a chain with three slender, golden keys. It looks like jewelry. I lift it in my hand and turn them over. The keys are big enough to be real, but something about them reminds me of the Tiffany's key pendants I've seen others wear over the past few years. I look for a tool mark or the 14K stamp, but there's nothing. Glancing around, I wonder what they unlock and why they're hidden. Whatever they unlock, it's not here. I return the keys to their hiding place, then return the drawer to the nightstand.

I head toward the front of the room and stop to stare at a pole. It has leather straps in three spots, one of which resembles a collar. In front of that is a wand on wheels. It's about three feet tall, adjustable, and has a clamp on the top. It goes with the pole, but I can't figure out what it does.

Mel's voice startles me. "You want a demonstration?"

"No."

Mel laughs, rolls the thing forward, and locks the wheels. "Adjustable, and there's a remote somewhere. You get tied to the post, locked in so you can't move, and the other person uses the remote with the correct toy on the end to either tease or make you come. I had a client who was into this shit. He had a shocking dildo he liked to use."

My eyes go wide as my girlie parts cringe. "Oh, God! Did it hurt?"

She shrugs. "Not really, but it's not my thing. Well, if I'd been the one calling the shots, it might be a different story. Black is into some messed up shit! Is that a bucking barrel?"

Mel walks over to a large, tapered cylinder with an O-ring on the front. It's upholstered in leather and sits suspended horizontally, elevated off the floor by an iron hydraulic frame. "Shit. This thing cost a fortune!" Mel runs her hand down the length of it, then knocks her fist against it, expecting to hear a hollow sound. Instead, it thuds like something is inside. She glances at me, "Wonder what's in here?"

Mel crawls underneath, finds a seam in the leather, pulls it apart, and shoves her hand into the barrel. She immediately pulls her arm out again, dumping a wad of cash on the floor. Her face lights up. "No fucking way! Black hid her cash in here?"

I look under and grin. "She put it in the one place no one would look."

"She forgot about us. This kinda thing makes most people want to run away. Not me. Been there. Done that. Literally." Mel reaches inside again and pulls out more cash. The third time she yanks out a black bag too. She sits up and opens it. "Damn. I could live off of the contents of this purse for the rest of my life."

"What is it?" I lean in, trying to see.

Mel folds the fabric open and offers it to me before leaning down and sealing the trap door on the bottom of the barrel.

I open the little sack and look inside. Something glints in the darkness. I tip the bag into my palm, and a collection of stones tumble out. "Diamonds! There are, like, three dozen in here."

"And they're big," Mel adds, straightening.

"Who would have paid her in diamonds?"

Mel gives me a look. "Who do you think? Which means Black has been doing shit she shouldn't do for a while. I wonder if she was into this shit while Vic's father was alive." Mel stops ogling the stones in my hand and glances at me. I put the rocks back in the bag, and she murmurs, "He's not your father, you know, and that junior asshole isn't your brother. Blood is just shit that runs through your veins, Avery. Don't let anyone tell you otherwise."

That makes me feel a little better, but it still makes my skin crawl to know I'm related to such evil people. There are no guarantees in life. None. It wouldn't bother me so much if I knew who I was turning into, but my identity slipped between my fingers the day I met Sean. It's not his fault. It's just timing. I would have been ensnared in all this with or without Sean. In a way, the insanity has brought me friendships that are stronger than blood—which is what Mel means.

I drop my head and sincerely tell her, "Thanks, Mel. You're as close to a sister as I could get."

She offers a wry smile and sniggers, "You just wish you were this tan!"

Arching a brow at her, I fold my arms over my chest. She's such a goofball. "I think you mean black."

"That, too. Then you could wear hoop earrings and be a badass like me. But you can't. You're the younger sis, the nerd, and way too pasty. It's all right," Mel covers my hand with hers. "I'll look out for you."

CHAPTER 7

~SEAN~

Nothing. Miss Black keeps her secrets close and her enemies closer. I thought I knew her well but never considered her capable of human trafficking. Kidnapping and enslaving people is so far removed from her original life goals that I wonder if she lied to me the entire time I knew her. It wouldn't surprise me now.

Survival instinct is strongest when a person is about to hit rock bottom. Miss Black isn't the type of woman to go down without a fight. Even so, this is so disturbingly wrong I don't know how to process it. It makes me wonder who is a more formidable opponent here—Black or Vic

Jr.? While getting shot by that bastard would suggest Vic, the silent involvement of Black makes me wonder if she's the brains behind the whole operation. In which case, unhinged or not, we should be more wary of her as our adversary.

My mind flickers back to my mother, singed and chained. Her filthy face and ripped nails didn't escape my notice. She was either in or near the mansion when the explosion occurred. Dirt and grime lined her nail beds and covered her forearms as if she'd been digging through the wreckage. She lost someone significant to her that day. Now the world thinks she's dead, and Black intends to sell her. She won't be bought for her body—anyone interested in acquiring Constance Ferro is her enemy. Mother wronged so many people it's impossible to choose who it could be, but I have a few hunches. The good thing is she's still locked in that room. No one jumped at the chance to buy her. The bad thing is she's still locked in that room. It's possible they were stalling to line up her sale.

Avery's compassion nearly made me stop and take Mother with us and damn the consequences. Regardless of the bad things Mother's done, this is a hideous way to die—being sold as property and losing all sense of safety, sense of self. That alone could unhinge her.

I rustle through papers on a hallway desk and hear Marty approach. He's silent, but there are telltale signs in the way he moves, in the noises of the house. A floorboard groans softly, and I don't turn as I speak. "Time to go?"

"Pull out. They're headed this way with Vic Jr. in tow. I'm supposed to be here for them so get the fuck out now."

"Got it."

Marty jogs down the hall, repeats his message to the girls, then melts into the shadows.

I want to free my mother, but that means revealing we're coming. It risks Avery, and I can't do it. I've played the scenario over and over again in my mind, trying to come up with an alternative, but I come up empty handed. There's no way to release my mother without giving us away. I can't jeopardize Avery. I won't lose her. I have to protect her. Even so, Pete will kill me if something happens to Mother. Jon will... Well, it's hard to predict how he'll react. Jon's still pissed at the world and hides it with a smile.

As I move down the hall, I meet up with the girls. Mel arches a brow at me and snorts. "You were into kinky shit before you met Black, weren't you?"

Avery gasps and whispers, "Don't ask him that! I haven't even asked him that!"

"Well, ask him! He's standing right here."

I repress the growl that's building in the back of my throat. "Ladies, we need to grab Henry and get out. I'm sorry it was for nothing. I can't believe we're leaving empty handed."

"We aren't." Avery's eyes gleam, and she tips her head toward Mel.

"We found a stash of cash and more. Check it." She holds up a baggie and tosses it to me. I slow, glance around a corner, then open the pouch and glance inside. Clear stones gleam within.

"Diamonds?" I'm surprised Black keeps them here. "Where were these?"

"In a practice bull along with a stash of cash." Mel holds up a handful of one hundred dollar bills.

"You took it?" I hiss, scolding her. I can't help it because it was an incredibly reckless, infantile move. "Removing those things could backfire. What if she notices they're gone?"

"There had to be a cool mil in there, along with a bunch of other jewel baggies. She won't miss one unless she inventoried before tonight." Mel shrugs. "Besides, this could make a big difference for a girl like me. I earned this and, if I don't get whacked tonight, I'm starting over again. This pouch will help me."

Avery reaches out, takes Mel's hand, and squeezes it reassuringly.

We're taking too long, and I feel my nerves fraying. "That's a lovely story, but we need to get the fuck out of here. Where's Henry?"

"Still in the computer room," Mel says, but as we step in front of the door, he's gone.

I swear and shove my hands through my hair. I need to get that moron out of here before he gets caught, but I don't know where he went. I shoot a text to Marty and continue shoving the girls toward the door.

My phone buzzes:

MARTY: HIDE. THEY ARE HERE.

"Shit." Something inside me snaps and clicks into place. I'm on autopilot. I usher the girls to the basement. Just as the back door opens, we're swallowed by the darkness, safe to observe several pairs of feet shuffling by, each making a distinct sound. The click-clack noise of Black's heels is easy to identify. The thick leather soles of Vic's shoes make a silent swish. The other men scuffle behind them, totaling eight.

A silver beam of moonlight cuts through the basement window, illuminating Avery's face. Her big brown eyes glance at me, near panic. She whispers, "What do we do?"

I shake my head and put a finger to my lips. Knowing Black, she has the entire place bugged.

Unless Henry left the security system in chaos mode, she'll see us. Cameras are concealed in the upper corners of the basement walls. I saw them in the security room when we entered the house.

Mel gestures toward the tiny windows leading to the side lawn. She tips her head and moves her eyes in a way that tells me exactly what she's thinking.

I nod silently and step closer, whispering so low it barely makes a sound. "I'll boost you up. Mel first, then Avery."

Avery turns toward me with her eyebrows knotted together. "What about you?"

"I'll be fine. Just go." My voice tells her this is not open for debate, so she doesn't argue.

Mel unhooks the latch and points to a spot in the shrubs. "Meet me over there, Avery. Sean, we'll see you back at Henry's."

I nod tightly and lift her with ease. Mel shimmies through the tiny window and rolls onto the grass. She rights herself and crouches as she slips into the shadows.

I step toward Avery, heart pounding as fear tries to take hold. I shove it down and swallow hard. As I grip her thighs and lift, she looks down at me, pleading.

"Don't make me leave you here. Sean, I can't—"

"You can. I'll be fine—especially if I don't have to worry about you. Meet me at Henry's. I'll see you soon. Go." I hold her up to the window ledge, waiting as she grabs hold and crawls out onto the lawn. She rolls on her side and looks down at me, worry filling her dark eyes.

She reaches back through the window and touches my cheek with her fingers. It's a soft caress, the kind I'd been afraid of before I met her. "Be careful."

Her eyes tell a different tale, swirling with anxiety so intense it's impossible to hide. Her neck is rigid, with every muscle corded tight. Her hand quivers slightly, but I don't comment. She's stronger than she thinks she is, and, when pushed, Avery turns into a tiger. She thinks she's some frail flower, doomed to wilt at the slightest difficulty. She couldn't be more wrong. Her ability to explore new things with me—like the tank, for example—show she's able to hold it together when she's most vulnerable. People like that are rare. She doesn't know the extent of her strength, not yet. When push comes to shove, she'll find out. The floodgates holding back that truth will strain and crack. Only then will Avery know who she is and what she's capable of, and not a moment sooner.

I take her hand and kiss her fingertips, mouthing, GO.

I step away and close the window as Avery fades into the inky black landscape. Mel is skilled with her knife, so if they get spotted before they're off the property, I expect she'll win. As long as a gun isn't involved.

I can't think about it. My stomach churns uneasily, and I move to the back of the room looking for a place to bunker down. That's when I hear the small whisper.

"Pssst." I glance around in the darkness, not seeing a thing, but I recognize the voice—the ridiculously feminine and formal call. It's Henry.

"Over here, you massive oaf." Henry leans out from under the staircase and waves me over. I duck underneath just as the lights flick on and flood the room. Henry lowers his gaze, blinking as he adjusts to the brightness seeping under the stairs.

The room is unfinished for the most part. The small space under the stairs has a concrete shelf to support the steep staircase above. Henry jerks his head to the side and climbs, shifting over to make room for me. I don't fit as easily as he does. I have to shimmy myself in place, stomach down on the cold cement, with my shoulder overlapping Henry's.

He glances up at me, murmuring, "Next time I'm the big spoon."

I punch him lightly in the kidney, and he winces. "Shut up," I hiss.

Voices carry down from the landing above, followed by the sound of footfalls creaking on the staircase, until several men are on the basement floor. I can see their ankles as they pass.

They're talking to one another, and I don't recognize any of their voices. "Why are we keeping the bitch? This is going to blow up in his face."

"You weren't paid for your brain, Gragg. Grab the barrel and lift on three. One. Two. Three."

Huffing, Gragg groans, "Even so, moving her is risky."

"These aren't for Ferro—they're for Vic's kid sister."

Ice shoots through my veins. I strain to hear more, as they move up the stairs.

"What's got him so obsessed with her anyway? She's a distraction," Gragg complains.

"Right, and the sooner she's gone, the better he can focus. So stop talking and lift the fucking barrel already."

Gragg curses and pauses before reaching the landing. "Got it. Get the girl, shove her in here, give her to the boss, and get more cash than we can spend. I'm down with that. It just seems like a waste of time."

"Since when is earning massive amounts of money a waste of time? Lift the goddamn barrel, and let's get the fuck out of here. The girl was spotted. We've got to grab her before she vanishes again. I'm not taking a bullet for that bitch, and Vic won't stop until he gets her, so let's move already."

Gragg protests, "Yeah, but I don't get it."

Several swearing voices scold Gragg simultaneously. He stops asking questions, and when the rest of the men are out of the basement, the room goes dark.

Henry whispers, "They're headed to my mansion to take Avery."

I was thinking the same thing. I shove off of Henry and fall on the floor, frantic to warn her. Rushing to the window, I peer outside. Marty is pacing with another man. Shit. I can't leave this way while they're standing there. I'll be spotted and shot.

Henry walks up behind me. "Thanks for your help back there, you lumberjack."

I tug at my hair and pace like a caged animal. I can't text Marty, and risk his life. At the same time, I can't get to Avery if they don't fucking move. I want to scream, but I can't. My heart races faster as I think about what they're going to do to her. Shoving her body in one of those oil barrels is going to make her nuts. She'll have to fold her body into a tiny ball and once they seal her inside—fuck. That will screw with her so that she won't have her wits about her when they dump her out in front of her asshole brother.

"We have to get out of here," I growl.

"Yes, I heard." Henry glances at the remaining barrels. "They took more than one. You realize that means they're planning on capturing several of us tonight. It's ironic we're all over here, and Vic is headed toward the mansion. He must have seen the article in the paper and recognized Avery."

I turn, drained of patience, and grab his shirt collar, squeezing hard. "Avery and Mel just took off in that direction, and, unless we stop them, they're fucked. Do you get that?"

Henry swats at me. "Yes. Kindly release me." I set him down, and the man smooths his shirt. He looks at the floor, then back at me. "There's something I can do."

"From here?"

"Yes, well, perhaps. It depends on if my drone is charged." Henry grabs his phone, and the little screen glows as he flips to an app and opens it.

I want to strangle him. "You denied owning a drone."

"Pish, posh." He waves a limp wrist at me. "I denied saying the drone shooting pictures of Avery was mine. I also stated my belief that drones are a pain in the ass, and that I don't appreciate being forced to register mine with the FAA. I never said I didn't have one."

I want to kill him. Glaring at the side of his head, I snarl, "You said exactly that."

He shrugs, "I exaggerated, and you should be glad. My little white lie may just save the girls." He taps in a series of commands and then stares at a live camera feed from the drone. It's inside a building, hovering by a window. "I liked that pane. It's handmade glass from an estate in Suffolk, you know."

"Henry—" I warn.

He smashes the drone through the window, and it's off into the night. The thing shoots up high and buzzes over the house before darting toward us. If Avery is still on foot, it might be possible to get to her first.

"Can you talk to her through the drone? I mean if you find her, how will she know it's you?"

He tucks his chin and represses a grin. "She won't be able to hear me, but she'll know it's from me."

"How?" Henry squirms, avoiding my gaze. I don't press him and change my line of questioning. "And then?"

"Then we get them to follow the drone away from the mansion."

"Mel is more likely to hit it with a bat than follow it."

"Perhaps, but once they glance at it—well, you'll see." Henry flies the thing around five hundred feet—low enough not to interfere with aircraft, but high enough that it can't be seen from the ground. A few minutes later, it's over Black's house, dropping like a stone from the sky. It stops, hovers above the ground, and pivots slowly near the trees where Avery was supposed to meet Mel, but they're already gone.

CHAPTER 8

~AVERY~

Mel shoves me forward. We've been crawling through bushes for way too long. I'm tired, and my body feels like it's made of bricks. I wish I could sleep for a few days, eat a ton of ice cream, and that this whole situation would be over. But it's not.

"I think we made a wrong turn somewhere." I stand upright and get bitchslapped by a spruce.

Mel chortles. "That was so funny! You should see the look on your face!"

"We're in the fucking Pine Barrens. We're going to fall into a pit and get mauled by bears." I frown and glance around, upset.

Mel waves me off. "That shit don't live here. Worst you'll find is the Jersey Devil."

I can't help it. I laugh. "I think he lives in Jersey, Mel."

She snorts, "And what? This can't be his summer home?"

"It's not summer!"

"Psh. Like that's a good reason. You need to broaden your mind. Since when can't a demon-spawned baby fly to his vacation residence in a season other than summer?" Mel rolls her eyes and shoves back a branch, marching on.

When she says baby, my heart pangs, as if the offspring of the demon were my child. I imagine it being misunderstood and crying as it tries to find me, but can't. I blink rapidly, chasing the story away. What the hell was that? Compassion for a demon baby? I'm going crazy. I must be.

I follow Mel even though I have no idea where we are or where she's going. I think she's lost, but I'm not entirely certain. It's so dark. The moonlight makes a lacy pattern on the forest floor, but it's difficult to see much else.

Mel stops short, her arms waving like mad. I grab her as she's about to fall forward. I didn't see it in the shadows, but perched on the edge it's clear there's a massive pit in front of us and if she doesn't regain her balance, we're going to fall right into it.

Heart pounding, I tug hard, and she falls back with me to the ground. Relieved, I gasp and lie on the forest floor for a moment before getting up. When we rise, we stand, step closer, and peer over the edge.

Mel's eyes go wide. "It's a fucking mass grave. I told you it was that freaky demon."

She sounds worried, but as I stare at the hole, I recognize what it is. "It's not a grave, Mel. It's a sand mine. Some asshole came out here to steal sand."

Her face crumples and she stares at me like there's a goat on my face. "Say what now? Who the fuck would steal sand? It's sand!"

"I know, but construction sites need sand. It's expensive, so they come out here, steal the sand from the Pine Barrens where no one lives or looks, and then backfill the hole with garbage when they're done." She blinks those golden eyes at me like I'm lying. "I'm not making this up. It's a thing."

"Looks like a mass grave to me."

"It's not."

"Mine's a better story."

"Yeah, it probably is."

Her eyes cut to the side as she glances at me, and then back at the pit. "So when we get a book deal, and they adapt the story into a movie, we're gonna say this was a mass grave."

"A movie?" I nearly laugh.

"Yeah, why not? Think about it." She starts talking with her hands, painting the air with the swipe of her palms. "We got intrigue, mystery, and a lunatic that puts that chainsaw guy to shame."

I frown. She's right. This entire thing is more messed up than any movie I've seen. "Fine, it's a demon grave."

"Psh, now that's ridiculous. Demons can't dig. They're not supernatural dogs. Geeze, Avery."

Something buzzes overhead and darts by, shaking the treetops. Little lights shine down and blaze their beams through the branches. It startles the crap out of me, and I scream and jump at Mel. She wasn't ready for it. She loses her balance, and we both tumble forward and slide to the bottom of the sand pit.

Mel swears a slew of words that make my ears ring and then shoves me off her prone body so she can stand. "You did not just shove us down into a demon grave."

I close my eyes for a second and explain, "There was a light—"

Mel hadn't noticed. She didn't look up—no one ever looks up. "You shoved us into a hole because of a lightening bug? Come on, Avery. Grow a pair." She walks toward the side and tries to climb out, but can't. It's too steep, and the walls aren't stable. Every time she gets a step up, the sand loosens, and she falls.

I stand up and brush off the sand. "It wasn't an insect. It was one of those weird helicopter things—a drone."

Mel growls and tries to climb out again, but only falls back into the pit. She stomps her foot and swears again. When she's finished with her tantrum, she glares in my direction, adding, "Thanks to you, we're trapped at the bottom of a goddamn hole! I'm not interested in playing the live version of Frogger right now."

"I think you mean Pitfall. And at least there's no demon spawn down here with us." I imagine how silly we must have looked falling in slow motion into the pit, arms flailing, bodies tumbling over each other before skidding to a stop at the bottom. My lips twitch, and I snort softly trying to swallow the giggles building inside of me, but a few pop out.

Mel glares at me while swatting sand off her arms. "It's not funny."

I can't stop. My chest shakes as I try to wipe the grin off my face and be serious. "Ok, I'm fine." I'm not. Laughter is still fizzing inside my chest, but it's no longer on my face.

"Good," she snaps. "What's the best way to get out of here?"

I glance around, "Well we could bounce across a few logs and hope we don't land on a gator by mistake." I make a Tarzan sound that sounds more like a bleating goat.

Mel glares at me, pissed at first, and then starts cracking up. She doubles over and puts her hands on her knees as she giggles so hard she can't breathe. "Holy shit! That sounded like the game! It was like you were half goat and half Tarzan." She straightens and points at me, "Do it again."

I make the noise once more, louder this time. My last bleat comes out choked as I nearly gag myself with laughter.

Mel is belly laughing, bent over and wagging a finger in my direction. "That's hilarious! Who knew you were a goat girl deep down inside!" Mel tries to make a bleating sound, but it comes out more like the ACK, ACK, ACK of a machine gun.

"Bwuhahahaha! Your goat lives in the ghetto and is packin' some serious heat, Mel. What the hell kind of farm animal sounds like that?" There are tears in the corners of my eyes from laughing so hard. I wipe them away as we finally get control of ourselves.

Mel lets out a long sigh through her mouth and looks over at me. "If it ain't some asshole trying to kill us, it's all fun and giggles—"

"Yeah, until we fell down a hole."

"Do you know how embarrassing this is? I'm like a knife ninja. In a street fight, I win. I always win. I can't believe I'm stuck in a fucking hole." She shakes her head and glances around.

"With me! It could be so much worse." Grinning, she flicks her gaze up to meet mine. "Seriously, Mel. I don't mind being trapped in a pit with you, but Sean is going to freak out."

She finally stops laughing and walks toward me in long, slipping strides as the sand moves under her feet. "Why couldn't we fall into a pit with a hot man? That Pitfall guy was hot, but he was a little too boxy and rectangular if you ask me." She says it so deadpan that I start giggling again. "Seriously, though. We couldn't fall into one of them holes that already has smashed up concrete in it and a ladder?"

"We're not lucky like that, Mel." I lean against the sidewall and slide down. I pull my feet in toward my chest and tip my head back. The night sky looks like spilled ink with a dusting of silver glitter to make up the stars.

Mel paces for a few turns and then sits next to me. "If I die in a hole, I'm gonna be pissed." She folds her arms across her chest and tips her head back, closing her eyes.

"Are you going to sleep?"

"Yeah, so?"

"What about demon babies and vacation homes?"

She swats a lazy hand at me. "It's not summer. Dude ain't here."

CHAPTER 9

Mel naps next to me while I stare at the sky thinking, wishing I could contain my thoughts, but they bubble up and overflow from my mind like a pot of boiling water. I can't stop it. Images flash rapidly through my head like a confused movie. The scenes don't blend and the timeline spirals in an illogical loop. Silent screams, slick skin, a diamond engagement ring, the cold feel of the gun grip in my hand, the hard ground at my parents' graves, and blood—pouring, pooling, covering my pale skin, tainting me. Fear intensifies and chokes me until I can't breathe. I jump up and chase the thoughts from my mind when the noise comes closer. It sounds like a giant bee.

I kneel next to Mel and shake her shoulder. "It's back."

Just as she stands next to me and we look up in unison, a bright light shines down directly overhead, blinding us. The drone loudly buzzes as it drops close to us way too fast. It stops at eye level and hovers in the air in front of us.

"I wish I had a bat," Mel growls at the machine, "I'd smack it!" She bends over and pulls up two fists of sand, ready to toss it into the four spinning propellers.

"Wait!" I grab her arms, stopping her and get closer to the drone. It's not white like the one I saw a few nights ago. This one is flesh-toned with brown streaks and—is that an eye? I get closer, blinking twice at the device before chills race up my spine and my stomach turns sour. "Tell me that's not what I think it is."

Mel leans in, careful not to get close to the spinning blades allowing the drone to hover. She snorts, "That crazy fucktard really has the hots for you. He made an Avery drone."

The drone is shrink-wrapped with a picture of me. I blink hard, hoping my face and body will disappear from the side of the machine. It's the picture I gave Henry of me way back before I knew he was insane. It was meant to stay in his wallet. I shouldn't be plastered to the sides of a drone.

Straight-faced, I stare at it with contempt. "That bastard. He made me a flying whore!"

Mel tries not to grin. She eyes the contraption carefully then spits out, "Damn, he's freaky. I bet he has a thing for Wonder Woman."

"I bet he has his own invisible jet. Screw Wonder Woman."

"That's what he said!" She chuckles and slaps her knee. "Damn, I'm funny!"

The drone tries to take off, and then circles back when we don't follow. It does the same thing four more times, trying to get us to take off after it. I shake my head and point, but they don't seem to get it.

Mel plucks the drone from the air, flips it over, and says slowly directly into the tiny camera on the bottom, "We can't follow. We're stuck in a pit." Then she tosses the thing up in the air, and it falls like a stone, almost hitting the ground before shooting into the treetops again.

She laughs. "I bet that made his British britches bunch. By the way, you don't want to see what's on the underside of that drone. He's a sick mofo." Her lips twitch like she wants to smile fondly. It's almost admiration. No, that's not quite right. There's a starry look in her eye combined with the almost goofy grin.

Wide-eyed, I point at her. "Holy shit! You like him!"

"I do not!" She scoffs, grimacing like it's an insane accusation.

"Yes, you do! You've got that bashful smile on your face, the one that's totally smitten and goofy! How could you like him? He's insane."

She doesn't argue this time. "I don't know. He's hot, funny, and a little sick. Besides, who are you to criticize? You're dating the world's most twisted guy."

Laughing darkly, I challenge, "Yeah, but Henry is worse."

She grins wolfishly and presses her palms together. "Yes, he is."

CHAPTER 10

I have no idea how much time passes, but it feels like hours by the time Sean and Henry show up. They stand at the rim with their hands in their pockets—their stances mirrored. Sean's head tips to the side and Henry's eyes are wide like he just realized he needs to dig a pit in his shed immediately.

I wave at Sean with the tips of my fingers. "Hey. How you doin'?"

He snorts and offers a lopsided grin. "How the hell did you end up in a hole?"

Mel glares at me, muttering, "Pasty, here, pushed us in when that sick bastard's drone buzzed us."

Sean and Henry are about to say something, but Mel cuts them off. Waving a pointer finger in the air she narrows one eye to a slit and growls, "And don't you give her shit about it. It's dark and freaky out here at night. There are worse responses to getting hit in the face with a robotic flying machine."

Jaw slackened, I gape at her. "You chewed me out!"

"Right," Mel looks at me and holds up a palm toward the guys, "which is why it'd be redundant at this point to do anymore scolding. I already took care of it. Plus, I don't like it when they yell at you."

"But it's okay for you to do it?"

She folds her arms over her chest and cocks her head to the side. "Damn straight."

I roll my eyes and look up at Sean, "Save me. Please." I lift my arms to him like a little kid, and he smiles, shaking his head.

"Hold on." He takes an armful of rope and ties it around a tree.

Henry stands at the rim and asks, "Is sand your Kryptonite, Melanie? Did you finally meet a foe you can't best?" He chortles to himself.

"Fuck you, Sweater Vest."

He glares coolly at her. "Sorry excuse for an assassin."

"Who the fuck says I'm a hit man?"

"Obviously, you're not. I'm rather disappointed." He smirks at Mel. I step back waiting for flames to erupt from her mouth. "If you were, you wouldn't be stuck in a hole."

"Asshole."

"I'd rather enjoy visiting your hole."

Mel's lips twist in disgust. "Yeah? Well, whip it out and let's see what happens."

Henry snort-laughs as Sean throws the rope over the edge and reminds him, "She's going to get out of that pit, and you'll wish you hadn't said a word."

Henry slips his hands into his pockets and laughs, throwing his head back like Sean is funny. It sounds forced and sarcastic. "As if."

I laugh and slap my hands over my mouth. Mel glares at me, so I rush to the edge where Sean tossed the rope over the edge. Looping my hands around the thick-corded rope, I tell her, "He sounds like you."

"He does not. He wishes he could sound as amazing as me. But he can't."

Henry waves his pointer finger through the air, throws out his hip, and sways his head—impersonating Mel. "He does so. He's much more amazing than me, and I'd love to shag the fucker."

I grin at Sean as he pulls me up. I shout to Henry, "You should've listened to Sean. Mel's going to rip your face off when she gets out."

Henry swats a hand at her. "She couldn't hurt a butterfly. Her peak is over. She's droopy, and headed for a gravity induced decline, am I right, love?"

After Sean pulls me over the top, I push up with my knees and stand, wiping the sand from my limbs. He looks down at me tenderly, tucking a strand of hair behind my ear. "Thank God you never do as you're told." He kisses my forehead and seems to breathe easier.

The moment I'm off the rope, Mel grabs it and scales the side of the pit, hurling her body over the rim before jumping up and rushing Henry. He stands perfectly still, his hands in his pockets and an indifferent expression on his face. His serene façade cracks just as she's about to plow into him. He lets out a shriek and runs, arms flailing, into the woods. Mel races after him, swearing up a storm.

Sean glances down at me. "Do I need to stop her?"

"Nah, she likes him."

Sean's eyes widen. "I'd hate to see what it looks like if she hates him."

"I know, right?" I sigh and lean into Sean.

He wraps his arms around me and kisses the top of my head as he tells me what he heard in the basement at Black's. "They know you're at Henry's. We can't go back there."

I cringe at the thought of the barrel. No, it's more than that. It terrifies me, shooting shards of ice through my veins, cutting all the way to my heart. I swear it stops beating for a moment. I pull away and turn toward Sean. "Then we can't wait. We need to head directly to Vic Jr.'s and finish this."

"There's a step in the middle first. You need to call Black and accept the job."

The lump in my throat grows to a gargantuan size, strangling me from within. There's so much pressure on me it feels like one wrong move will mash my body to the pavement. One false step and I'm dead. No, it's worse than that—my sick brother has a barrel with my name on it.

I nod and whisper, "If he catches me… If this doesn't go right—"

Sean pulls me into his chest, wrapping his strong arms around me. "I won't let him hurt you. Not now, not ever. After tonight, Vic Jr. will be sorry he ever fucked with a Ferro."

CHAPTER 11

The phone rings and Black answers, "Avery, I'm surprised to hear from you."

I'm breathing too fast, and my voice is trembling. She'll hear it, so I do the only thing that would make those sounds seem reasonable. I sniffle and blurt out, "I want the job. The madam job you offered before."

"What about Mr. Ferro? I thought you were through with the matchmaking business?" Her voice is silky and smooth. I can picture her sitting at her desk with a smile on her face. The game of cat and mouse has always amused her. She's going to toy with me for a while before making her final decision.

My throat is tight, and I'm shaking, I answer tersely, "He left me." My voice rings hollow. "You said he'd do it. You told me—" I sniffle and gasp, "You told me he'd leave, and he did."

"I hadn't heard Mr. Ferro returned home. When did this occur?"

"I don't know! He walked away earlier and said his life here is toxic. Miss Black, I really don't want to talk about him."

"So he left on his jet this evening?"

"I guess so." I know so. Correction—I know his jet mapped their flight plan and took off with one passenger this evening. If she checks, she'll be able to corroborate my story. "I need that job, Miss Black. Is it still open?"

She pauses, sighs deeply, and responds. "It is, but considering your behavior—the way you disregard every rule and refuse my oversight—Avery, this position isn't for you. Some women were made to lead while others are better working on their backs."

I mash my lips together and try not to scream at her. "Give me a chance. I'll show you how valuable I can be. I'm not interested in men anymore. I'm never falling for another guy as long as I live. I have nothing else to do, no other source of income. Miss Black, please..." I beg, adding a jagged breath at the end to sound like I'm not quite done crying.

"Never beg," she scolds. "It shows weakness."

"Yes, Miss Black." Silence passes between us, stretching on forever.

I start to think she's walked away from her phone when she replies, "Be here at 11 pm. You can shadow me this evening. I'm speaking with a potential client. If he signs, he pays up front. We go in, collect his contract and preferences, pictures, and then make the match. He has a girl on his arm within twenty-four hours. That's how it works. Are you sure you're ready for this?"

My heart pounds like I've never wanted anything more. Miss Black is a master manipulator. It's no wonder she's so good at this. If I didn't know what I was walking into, I would have shown up with a smile on my face, grateful for her help. I sound as earnest as possible when I answer, "Yes, God, yes! Thank you, Miss Black. I won't let you down."

"No, you won't."

I hang up and turn to Mel. Henry is behind her, digging through abandoned boxes in the basement of the dorm. We had no other place to go—at least nowhere Black didn't know to look. And if Sean is spotted, they'll realize I know what's going on.

Mel is watching me with her golden eyes, nodding, silent until I hang up. Then she throws her arms around me and squeezes so hard my eyeballs nearly pop out of my head. "That was fucking perfect. There's no way she suspects a thing." Just as she releases me, Mel's cell rings. She nods for everyone to be silent and answers, "Hey, what's up?"

Miss Black's velvety voice seeps into the room through the phone. "I need you tonight."

"I've already got plans—" Mel's lips tip up at the corners.

"It's in your best interest to show up here. I have a client interested in your mark. I need you to ensure delivery. You know how Avery can get."

Mel interrupts, repeating, "I'm sorry, Miss Black, but I have other plans tonight."

She growls, her words dripping with unsaid threats, "I'll make it worth your while, and, if you look the other way, I believe we can reach a mutually beneficial arrangement. If you disregard your duties, however, I'll send Gabe after you, and you will not like his methods of persuasion. I suggest you show up here at 11 pm on the dot."

Mel pales slightly. "Yes, Miss Black. I'll be there. Hey, what's the plan? Some guy wants to rent her or what?" Mel tries to get Black to talk, and waits on edge—hoping she'll say something.

Black's not a fool, though. "Come and see for yourself," she says. "There's a lot more money to be made if you're willing to blur the lines, Melanie. Don't be late." The line goes dead.

Mel tucks her phone back into her pocket and glances at me. "I don't like this. Too many things can go wrong. I'd feel a lot better about it if Vic Jr. had a gun to his head the entire time."

Sean is tense, his jaw locked tight, and his thick arms folded over his chest. His chin is tucked low, and he's been thinking, not saying much until that moment. "There are a lot of variables, I agree, but as soon as you and Avery are inside and within range of his security system, we can move in. No one will walk away from this."

A box topples, and we look over to see a startled Henry holding up some Mardi Gras beads. "What?"

Mel snaps at him. "Are you even listening? This is it. We succeed, or we die. There's nothing in the middle."

"Yes, yes, I'm well aware." He stuffs the beads in his pocket and saunters over to stand next to Mel. "Marty is already on the premises to provide us a head start. He can make sure everyone is contained in the correct room at the correct time."

I feel sick, but I have to ask. "Are we going to slaughter all these people? No one walks away?"

Sean glances at me from under his lashes. "They decimated my home and tried to eradicate my entire family. They have my mother chained and plan on doing the same to you—or worse. We know Vic has plans for you, so you tell me— who gets to live? I'll bend to you on this, but letting any of these people walk away today leaves the possibility of losing more lives in the future. I prefer not to take that risk."

Mel asks, "What about Black? She's not even going to be there."

"She dies." Sean's voice is cold and resolute. "We find her after this, and end it."

Mel nods, says nothing. An icy calm overtakes the room, as we all stand there, none of us ready to do this. Mel finally says, "I need to shower and change. Hopefully, this is the last time we ever have to stand in front of Black for anything."

CHAPTER 12

Mel walks over to a rack in the back of the storage room draped with a plastic garment bag. She unzips the side and flicks through a few dresses before selecting something simple. It's a black cocktail dress with a low neckline, spaghetti straps, and a tulip skirt that falls mid-thigh on Mel. On me, it'd hang to my knees.

Mel tips her head to the side indicating I should pick something out. "Go on. I know you don't have a stash anywhere."

"Thanks, Mel."

"Sure." Her tone is dark, intense, "Make sure you can run in whatever you pick out. I want to strap a knife to you, too." She flicks her gaze at Sean, and he nods. Mel wasn't asking. It's as if she suspects things won't go as planned, and, of the lot of us, I'm the weakest link. Henry can buy his way out of trouble. Mel's a street fighter. Sean is Sean. Marty is a black ops agent. Gabe's a cop. I've got no real defensive skills, and the center of my chest aches because I wouldn't be standing here with these people if I did. If I could hold my own, I'd be a different person.

Mel's gone without another word. We can't even hear her footfalls as she wanders down the hall. That woman is part cat. I rush after her, calling out, "Mel wait."

I rush out of the storage room and find her at the end of the hall, waiting. "What?"

"I've never done anything like this before." I jog up next to her and sigh. "With the knife—what's the best way to use it to take someone down?"

"Avery, if you pull that knife then you strike to kill. There's no other option. You can't use it as a threat or you'll end up with a bullet in your head."

I swallow hard and feel my gut twist. Wringing my hands, I look her in the eye and shake off the pinpricks of fear crawling up my back. I throw my hands down to my sides, refusing to be afraid. "I don't intend for it to be a threat. I need to know. What do I do?"

Mel's tiger-eyes sweep over me as if deciding something. She holds out her brush in her right hand, pretending it's a knife. "You want to hold it like this. There will be more force in your blows. You can't hold back a damned thing. If the blade hits bone—it's around the entire ribcage—then you lose. It's that simple. Use your body, not just your arm." She shows me a few ways to fend someone off. "But when the shit hits the fan, and you have seconds to live, you aim for the weak spots, striking them hard and fast." She points to a few spots on my legs where the knife would do the most damage, then demonstrates how to avoid the spray of blood if I kill someone. "You may have more than one attacker, and if you get hot blood in your eyes, you're dead. Get it?" Her words sound clipped, like the conversation itself is painful.

I nod. "Mel, I'm—"

She steps in my face, and I back into the wall with a thud. "If you apologize, I'm going to bitchslap you. Fault and blame don't matter. It's a war, and you're the prize. If they live, you don't. There's not a fucking thing to be sorry about."

Mel steps back and glances to the side. After a moment of silence, she opens her mouth like she wants to say more, but thinks better of it. Mel shuts her mouth and stalks off down the dark hall, disappearing from sight.

CHAPTER 13

I grab a dress, perfume, makeup, and anything else I need to get ready for tonight. I'll either succeed or die in the outfit I choose for this evening. I want to feel powerful, so I take out the dress that speaks to me. It's a clingy white sheath reaching just below my knee. The fabric stretches so I can move. The front neckline gently swoops and flows over my shoulders into a deep V, extending past the small of my back. Twin straps keep the loose cloth securely in place.

After I tug it on, shimmying through the snug hips, I turn and jump. Sean is standing in the doorway to the girl's shower, his eyes dark. The intense look on his face makes my skin prickle.

He doesn't move. He remains in the threshold, frozen.

"Sean?" I say his name softly and pad barefoot toward him, stopping a step short of touching him.

The muscles in his neck and jaw are tense despite his casual stance. If I didn't know better, I'd think he was afraid. Sean tips his head to the side, leaning it against the doorjamb. "I could hide you."

I turn and walk back to the counter where I have my hairbrush, blow-dryer, and makeup spread out. I lift the brush and pull it through my wet hair. "I don't want to live like that, Sean, jumping at every sound. As it is, I barely sleep."

His voice is deep, gentle. "This will change you, Avery. If you make it to the other side, the woman looking back at you in the mirror will no longer exist."

"It's a necessary risk." I say the words, but they ring hollow. Sean's right, but I can't accept it. I don't even want to think about it.

"You only say that because you have no idea what it's like to live on the other side."

Turning on my heel I squint at him, annoyed. "Yes, I do. I've already murdered someone. Remember? Maybe it was nothing to you, but it still makes me sick."

He steps toward me, his firm body towering over mine. "That's what I mean. You killed him with a gun, and you feel this way. Imagine if you kill with your hands. That sensation never goes away. It'll haunt you for the rest of your life."

I turn back to the mirror, and pull the brush through another section of hair, detangling it as I go. "It's a necessary risk."

Anger flashes in his eyes. "That's bullshit."

Something inside me snaps and I round on him, pointing the brush at his face as I spew out sharp words. "Bullshit? Bullshit! You know what's bullshit? Leaving a person you care about trapped in the hands of two sociopaths!"

Sean flinches as if slapped. "My mother? You're mad about that?"

"No, I'm not mad. I'm disgusted. I can't fathom leaving my parents behind for any reason ever—even to save you. And if I was ever pushed to make such a sickening decision, I sure as hell would have been more torn up about it!"

He's in my face, hissing, "You think it doesn't bother me? You think that decision didn't rip me apart?"

"No, you barely looked at her!"

Sean's eyes soften. His voice becomes tempered, even. "She's alive, Avery. It shocked the hell out of me. Then again, it doesn't. Do you know why I was able to walk away?"

"You shouldn't have left her there." I try to turn away, but he grabs my arm tightly and yanks me in front of him.

Growling, he locks his eyes on mine, his body ready to fight, "I left her there because it's entirely possible all this shit fell this way because of her—that she's one of them."

My jaw drops as I gape at him, unable to speak.

Sean tugs my arm, snapping, "Don't give me that look."

My lips quickly curve into a sneer. "Sean, how could you say that?"

"How could you miss it? She's a snake and always has been. Human nature isn't that complicated, Avery. My mother will do what she's always done—watch out for herself. She doesn't give a flying fuck about you, me, or anyone but herself. That's a truth I accepted a long time ago. It's something you don't seem to understand, and I'm not going to let you find out the hard way that my mother is a sadistic bitch."

I try to pull my arm away and stomp on his toes, but Sean holds my wrist tighter. I wind up and pitch my hairbrush at him, but he deflects it, letting the thing clatter to the tiled floor. The yellow lights above pulse slowly like a generator kicked on. Sean pushes me back to the cold tile wall and pins me in place. His gaze is hungry, desperate.

"Tell me you trust me. With everything, not just sex." He leans his body into mine, crushing me. He's so warm, so tense. His scent fills my lungs as I try to twist away and shove him off, but I'm trapped. His sapphire gaze won't leave my face even though I attempt looking somewhere else. When I don't reply, he lifts his arm and presses his forearm across my chest and then slides it up to the base of my neck.

He watches me, knowing I hate the sensation of being trapped. Sweat forms on my brow, and it's getting harder to breathe under his weight. "Avery, say it. I need to know either way."

I close my eyes and turn my face away from him. He releases me, and I spring, full charge, rushing at him, pushing him back into the sink so that he trips backward. I grab the hot curling iron and hold it over his face, pinning him with his back arched backward until his shoulders touch the counter.

"It's not nice to make people tell you things they want to keep private." I feel crazy. Where is this coming from? What the hell am I doing? It's like my emotional compass exploded and ruined my ability to think.

Sean's shock flutters away after a moment. When he looks away from the hot rod just above his eyelash and glances at me, barely breathing. "When other people depend on you, facts make a difference. If I knew how tonight would play out, I wouldn't press you, but I don't know a goddamn thing. Unless you're going to burn me, I suggest you put that down right now."

I don't know why I do it. Something inside me is screaming at him, telling him how I feel. My hand moves as I shout, "I'm not weak!"

Sean's back is bent at an unnatural angle, making it hard for him to free himself without falling. When the curling iron comes at him, he sweeps his leg to the side and knocks me off-kilter. That second gives him the upper hand. The scalding iron brushes his cheek for half a second before he rips the plug from the wall and throws it across the room. It clanks and falls to the floor somewhere in the shower stalls.

He swipes away all the crap I have laid out on the tile slab, and it goes flying before he lifts me. His eyes are so deep, so lost. He sets me onto the countertop gently. An angry red burn lines his face where the curling iron kissed his cheek.

"I know you're not weak. That's not what I think at all. Please tell me you know that."

"I don't know what you think about anything. You never tell me—"

He presses a finger to my lips, silencing me. He leans in close, his mouth a breath away.

"You're the strongest woman I know. You're a survivor. You won't let anyone dictate your life. You never give up. You never surrender. I suspect your mantra is something about glitter and dying while fighting for your beliefs. Avery, the very last thing I would ever think about you is that you're weak." His voice is smooth, calming, and perfect. His words send shivers over my skin, each one falling like a gentle caress.

My eyes get glassy, and I blink a few times and ask, "Then why?"

"Why what? Tell me what you're asking, baby, because I don't know. I'll tell you anything. Ask me."

"Why did you pick me?" I squeak out. "You could have had anyone."

There's a pause, and then he lets out a long sigh and presses his forehead to mine. Looking into my eyes, he whispers, "I wonder the same thing about you. Why did you choose me? You could have had anyone."

"While that's flattering, it's not an answer. Sean, please. Tell me. I need to know."

"I picked you—I want you—because you're at a point in life where everything is changing. I admire your spunk, your optimism, and your hope. The way you smile and laugh like none of this shit that's going on is remarkable. The world could be going to hell around you—and it has—

and you still smile. Through all of it, you still care. That's what frightens me, Avery. Tonight is different. You're walking into this mess knowing you'll have to kill. It's different. It'll erase that smile, and it'll never come back."

My lips press together over and over in a nervous expression caught between a sorrowful smile and hope. "I believe you. I know that could happen. I know I'll change, and I want you to be there with me. You've been through this, and you came back. Sean, you can save me in more ways than one."

"Avery, not with this."

"I know you can bring me back because I did it for you. It's possible."

"Avery…" His lips are a breath from mine.

"I trust you, with everything."

I tangle my fingers in the hair at the nape of his neck and tip his head back as I pull him to me. When his mouth lands on mine, I kiss him softly, licking his lips in soft, steady strokes, closing my eyes and savoring everything about him. His strong hands slide up my back, pressing against the bare skin above my dress. He sweeps his hand under the fabric and cups my ass, pulling me toward him as the kiss deepens.

Sean moans into my mouth, and I wish we had more time, time to fight, time to get tangled in the sheets, and time to explore all the wonder that is Sean Ferro. But we don't. It's possible one of us will live, while the other will die tonight. I'm painfully aware I might not have the chance to hold him again. Sean must be thinking the same thing, because he moves his hands down my sides and to the hem of my dress, pushing it up my thighs so he can stand closer to me. His kiss deepens, and I realize this is the Sean I wanted so badly. It's the man lost between darkness and light—the man always fighting to be free. I have him here in this moment. I have the tender touches, combined with the forceful movements that make my heart pound.

My body heats up, reacting to his touch. His tongue in my mouth makes me purr, and I tip back my head wanting more, but Sean pulls away. He holds me tightly for a moment, crushing my face to his chest, cupping my head.

"If I lose you... I can't—" his words are barely audible, and then they choke off.

I grab his wrists, pulling them down to the counter, and shifting my weight until I'm pinning him there. It forces his face and those sad eyes to meet mine. "You won't lose me. Not tonight. Not ever. And if something happens, if we're parted for a little while—"

Sean shakes his head, "Avery, no—"

"Sean, promise me. Say it. Tell me you won't slip back into the monster. This is you. That man, the terrifying one, isn't you. You care. You still do—I feel it." I smile softly at him and release my grip on his wrists before leaning in. I unbutton his Oxford shirt and press my lips to his chest. Sean doesn't stop me. He doesn't ask me not to do it. That gentle kiss over his heart, over what he considers his weak spot, speaks volumes. I lift my head and look him in the eye. "Promise me."

"I promise. Forever and always. I'll hold on, but you have to do the same. You can't slip into the abyss. It will call to you, and you have to say no. If I'm not here, promise me you'll keep going, keep smiling." His breath is warm, pouring over me as he speaks. His tone is somewhere in between, and I wonder if this was his voice before his life became overrun with shadows.

"I promise."

I watch him for a moment, and when his lips come down on mine, I part my lips and let him kiss me deeply. His hands clasp my back as he pulls me to him, pressing his body against mine. As he tastes my mouth, swirling his tongue with mine, I arch my back, thrusting against him, wishing I could have more. There's not time for this. Mel is going to come looking for us in a moment. As it is, I'm already late.

I stop thinking, and toss aside the worry that's been making my insides twist with fear. I reach for his pants, loosening the buckle before unbuttoning his jeans and lowering the zipper. Sean's lips move to my neck as I free his hard length. I take him in my hand and feel his hot skin in my grasp. I slide my hand over him again and again, before pulling him toward the V at the top of my legs. I flick the G-string out of the way and guide him to the right place.

Sean lifts his head from my neck and watches me guide him. His lips part as he makes the most sinful sigh I could imagine. We're never this tender, this soft. I don't want him to hold back. As soon as he's in the right spot, I grab his ass with both hands and slam into him. His shaft slips deep inside me, and I gasp, throwing my head back. Sean remains still as I wrap my ankles around his waist and thrust against him, bucking my hips to his, fucking him hard.

After a moment, I cry out with a small climax and hold onto him, pulsing as I come back down. That's when Sean takes over. He rocks against me slowly, pressing in deeper, splaying my legs further before he lifts me off the counter and leans against the wall. Looking into my eyes, he thrusts in, pushing, holding himself there.

He whispers in my ear, grinning wickedly, "Let me do it." He moves his hips slowly, teasing me, making me want more.

I have no idea what he's talking about, but the urge to wildly buck against him is becoming hard to ignore. "Do what?"

He pushes into me and whispers in my ear, "I want to make you come. Let me." His voice is deep, a commanding tone that makes me wonder what he wants to do. I nod, and he moves me again, back to the long counter at the back of the shower stalls. When school was in session, girls sat in front of this long mirror to do their hair. Sean settles me back on the counter and then grabs my ankles, pulling me to the edge. My dress rolls up to my waist, showing my tiny panties. Sean hooks his thumbs around them and yanks them off, lifts them to his nose and inhales. The intimacy of the action makes butterflies erupt within me. They flitter from my fingers to my toes, making me feel light and loved. Then Sean offers a wolfish grin, pockets my panties and holds my ankles over my head. He pushes down his boxers and frees his dick, before pressing it against my core.

I suck in a loud breath and moan. He's hard, hot, and I want him so badly that I wriggle. His hand comes down on my butt, making it sting. "Don't move."

I try hard to stay still as he teases me harshly, moving his dick over my sensitive parts, but not slipping inside. I groan and try to dig my nails into the countertop, begging him. His voice makes me open my eyes. "Avery, look in the mirror while I fuck you."

I glance at him for a moment then turn my head to the side. I can see him, see me. My ankles are by his ears, clasped in his tight grip. He pushes into me slowly, taking his time about it. My mouth falls open into an "O," and when I forget about the mirror and look back at him, there's a sharp sting from his hand slapping me.

"Only look in the mirror," he growls, thrusting harder this time.

It's so hard to keep my eyes open, but I do. I watch through lowered lashes as he fucks me on the countertop, thrusting hard and pushing deep. The look on his face, the way his back arches with each thrust is divine. I want to lick every inch of him. Sean's eyes are on me as I keep my eyes on the mirror.

He breathes, "The expressions you make are beautiful. Don't close your eyes." He presses into me hard and then pulls out a little, slamming into me deeper this time.

I coo, feeling the smile on my face before I see it. I adore him. The look says as much. My lashes are lowered, and the corners of my mouth are tipped up. My hands are close to my neck, fingertips twirling a curl.

Sean rocks into me, developing a pattern that makes me crazy. It's almost like he's teasing me on purpose, but his dick is deep within me. Even so, I want more. I wish I could feel him deeper. I whimper, and he shifts my ankles and presses them back, folding me in half. He presses them to the counter and smiles. "You're limber."

"It's a good thing, too."

"Yes, it is." He kisses the tip of my nose, before asking, "Would you mind holding these?"

I can't help it, I grin. "So you can do what?"

"Fuck you senseless."

"I guess so." I hold my ankles next to my head and then everything changes. When he pushes in this time he's so much deeper, pressing in a delicious way that makes me cry out. I beg him for more, and he indulges me, thrusting harder, fucking me deeper. He rocks into me, over and over again, teasing me, pulling halfway out and then thrusting hard. He fucks me like that as I watch my face in the mirror. My eyelids are heavy, and my mouth is in a constant O begging for more. I have no idea what I'm saying, but I coo and whimper as he fucks me and, when I can't stand it anymore, he drives into me rapidly until I feel something deep within. The orgasm hits me hard and fast. Before I realize what happened, Sean drops to his knees and buries his face between my legs, lapping up my come in slow wet strokes. I cry out, clutching the counter. My legs shake and fall open because I can no longer hold them in place. As my body pulses, Sean presses his tongue inside me, licking, tasting, and touching me until I'm completely sated.

When he lifts his face, his scruff is glistening. He grins at me. "You're perfect." He backs away from my legs and stands. Then he leans over me, kisses me lightly, and holds up my panties. "I'm keeping these by the way."

I feel so fluffy and light. I have a dorky smile on my face when I ask, "Why?"

"To remind me that sex with you is better this way."

I prop myself up on an elbow and inquire, "And what if I want to be scared senseless and fucked hard? Who should I ask to do me then?"

Sean rushes at me, tickling me and scoops me up like I weigh nothing. "Me, always ask me to fuck you. I'll do anything you want, any way you want. I'm just saying that this kind of sex isn't off the table. Actually, fucking you on a table would be a lot of fun, too." He swings me around and then puts me on my feet. My legs feel like jelly, and I wobble for a moment, holding onto his waist and wishing I could bury my face in his crotch for a good long while.

I suck in my lip and look up at him. Sean grins. "You're perfect, completely, fucking perfect. Never change, Miss Smith."

"I wouldn't dream of it, Mr. Jones."

CHAPTER 14

Sean dresses, eyeing me with a wicked expression on his face. He pulls on his black jeans, wiggles into that tight sweater, and tops them off with a black trench coat. I smile at him and pull on the fabric at his waist. "Where'd you get this?"

Sean smiles boyishly. "Marty. He said one of Vic's regulars wears this thing, and I'd be less noticeable in it. Henry has one too. Do you like it?"

"Maybe if you were naked underneath." I grin up at him and kiss his lips softly. I pull away, wishing we had more time.

"I'll see you later."

"You know it." I smile as he walks away, feeling my chest constrict until I can't breathe. We both act like things will all work out, but if I've learned anything, it's that there are no promises in life.

***

My heart won't listen to my head as I drive my old car toward Miss Black's office. This is the last time, the last thing I have to do to be free from her and Vic Jr. This will be the end of it. I just have to survive. Freedom is an enticing goal. People have fought for it, died for it. Generations upon generations of people had it worse than me. I don't pretend to be leading a revolution. I'm not that girl. I'm pretty sure I'm not this girl either, but at this point, I only have two options—die or fight back. So I clutch the steering wheel until my knuckles ache and veer through traffic until I roll to a stop in front of a pharmacy. The butterflies in my stomach have razor sharp wings and slice me up from within. I'm ready to puke again, but it has nothing to do with Black.

I rub a hand over my stomach in a soft motion. It hasn't escaped me that I've felt tired and nauseous for the past few weeks. It seems to be getting worse, not better. I'm not stupid. I know what it means. I know it's not stress. But I want proof. I need to know for certain.

I exit the car, head into the store, walk down an aisle, and pluck an early pregnancy test from the shelf. Heart pounding, half wanting it to be true and half dreading the thought of going through tonight with a baby in my belly, I head toward the register. By the time I checkout, my eyes are glassy.

The cashier is in her thirties, sloppy red hair swept up into a bun and impaled by a pencil. She smiles at me. "You look beautiful."

I glance up at her. "Thank you." My face is pinched with worry.

She takes pity on me, tipping her head to the side while saying, "There's a restroom in the back. It's usually reserved for staff only, but it's yours if you want. No one will bother you back there. It's just Tina and me tonight."

"Thank you. I appreciate it."

She nods curtly, lowers her head and walks with determined strides toward the back of the store. I follow her with my item concealed in a plastic bag. We shove through a door and then into a breakroom. There's a small bathroom at the back. She turns on the light and smiles kindly at me.

"Life is challenging to live and even harder to plan. You can do it, though. Hang in there." She clasps my shoulder, and I nearly break down sobbing, only managing to hold it together by not answering.

I nod at her, slip into the bathroom and shut the door. I have to be pregnant. I'm completely insane. Kindness is making me sob, and if I see another baby lotion commercial, I'm going to buy stock in Kleenex. I don't wait. I don't linger and look at the box. I rip the sucker out, read the directions, and after doing everything right, I wait.

I fold my arms over my chest at first and look at myself in the mirror. My thumb is between my lips, and I'm ready to chew my nails off. I want to skip, holler, cry, and laugh all at once. As I stand there and watch the control box light up my heart pounds harder. Eventually, my hands wrap around my middle, and I hold on tightly, waiting, watching. There's a hole in the center of my chest that will fill with warmth if it's positive. I can feel it. Accident or not, I want this baby. I would never have had the guts to plan a pregnancy and welcome a little life into the world. Not in a million years.

My stomach sours as I wait and watch. It's two minutes of torture. Two minutes of surfacing dreams, things I'd never say, wishes I never dreamed before now. My nails dig into my arms as I turn away from the test. So far there's no second line, nothing. I can't stand looking, watching and seeing nothing happen. Maybe I'm not pregnant at all. Maybe it's stress going totally batshit crazy. I want to cry. I feel like I lost the baby I never had. A tear rolls down my cheek, messing up my makeup.

"Stop crying," I scold myself aloud. "There are other, more pressing things happening tonight. Focus, Avery!" I suck in a deep breath of air, straighten my spine and turn to pick up the test and throw it in the trash.

When I glance down at the piece of plastic, there's a second line.

I'm pregnant.

CHAPTER 15

I gasp, and it turns into a happy squee. I giggle and pick up the stick I peed on and jump up and down. I want to tell someone, but I can't tell Sean yet. We have to get through tonight first. There's a good chance I won't make it out of this and he will. He'll survive because he always has. I believe that. I have to believe it or go nuts thinking about the alternative. I couldn't let him go through losing a child again. He'll die inside. The monster will consume him, fully this time.

I yank open the door and beam at the clerk. "I'm pregnant." My voice is shaking, and my hands tremble. I'm still holding the stick like it's a bar of gold.

She smiles, full wattage at me. "Congratulations! You're going to be a great mom. I can tell how much you want this baby. It wasn't planned, was it?"

I shake me head. "Not at all. I'm on the pill. I'm not sure what happened."

She shrugs. "Life happens unexpectedly sometimes."

I love that song. I nod at her. "Yes, it does."

CHAPTER 16

Holy shit. There's a baby inside of me. A
baby! This can't be happening. I'm so excited I
can't think. I fly to Black's and realize I need to
slow down and focus. She cannot know about
this. Ever. I need to be a cold businesswoman,
just like her. If Black doesn't believe me, if she
isn't certain I'm done with Sean and will do
anything for whatever comes next, I'm
screwed—we all are. I let out one more baby
squee and lock the thought in the back of my
mind along with a bunch of other things I can't
deal with right now.

This part of the plan weighs heavily on my
shoulders, crushing me. I roll to a stop in front of
Black's office building.

"You can do this, Avery. You can do this," I chant, not really believing. I yank on the rearview mirror, intending to give myself a more elaborate pep talk. It comes off in my hand. I look down at the plastic clip on the back and flip the mirror over in my palm. The glass shines up at me, and I start laughing. Even though Sean repaired and restored this car from bumper to bumper, it still had an original part. I smile to myself and sink back in my seat.

My life has taken a wild tangent, flying into territory I would never have dared to glance at, leading me to walk into a war zone as the prey and the prize. No wonder why Mom was always frantic. They hid this from me so well that I never had a clue. Dad always made sure we were under the radar and Mom was a mom. What more could a kid ask for?

Leaning forward in my seat, I place the mirror on the dashboard and run my hand over my tummy one last time thinking it's a girl. It must be. I can feel it, which makes no sense.

I say to the baby, for the first time and possibly the last, "You and I won't run. We won't hide. We'll be free from all of this. I promise you that."

Determination I didn't know I possessed flows up my spine, straightening me, filling me with courage. I will survive. I'll get through this. I have to do it. For her.

***

When the elevator doors open, Gabe is there. He's in his black suit and white shirt. A dark tie is knotted around his neck, and his well-worn shoes are freshly shined. He nods at me, and presses a button with one beefy finger, taking us to the top floor.

"Good evening, Miss Stanz."

"Hey, Gabe." I stand with my shoulders back, eyes straight ahead.

He says nothing about Mel or Sean. Nothing about tonight's plan, but I know he has my back. I nod at him when the doors slide open, then exit the elevator. In long sleek strides, I pace across the floor, passing empty desks, and walk straight into Black's office without knocking.

"Hello, Miss Black." I speak with authority, with confidence I didn't feel until a few moments ago.

She's at her desk, annoyed I entered unbidden. "Avery, your manners could use work."

"As could yours." I'm clutching my purse in front of me and tip my chin up.

Black offers a half smirk and rises. A red dress hugs her slender form, scooping at the neck, and following her figure down to just below her knee. A thick gold chain hangs around her neck with three decorative keys dangling on the end. Each is a different shade of gold—yellow, white, and rose gold. One key is simple, plain, while another has diamonds glittering along the shaft. They're the keys from her nightstand, the set hidden in the secret drawer. Her lips are blood red. Coupled with her angular features, dark eye makeup, and dark hair, she's immaculate. No better than that. Miss Black always looks better than everyone. She prides herself on it.

She arches a perfectly plucked brow as she saunters toward me, her slender arms loosely folded across her ample chest. "Did we grow a backbone?" She stops in front of me, looks down into my face less than a foot away.

"Perhaps it was there all along." I'm careful not to smirk and repress my emotions, hiding them. They'll fuck me over royally. I have to be cold, mirror her exactly. She needs to think I like her, that I want to be like her. She needs to believe it wholeheartedly.

Black laughs lightly. "I would have seen it."

"I know you did." I step closer to her and meet her intense gaze. Black isn't the type of woman you fuck around with. She'll wipe the floor with me if I piss her off. There's a fine line between confidence and arrogance. I hope I'm on the right side because eating carpet doesn't sound appealing. "You saw it in me from day one. You knew my potential, and you called me out. I was the fool who denied it."

Black inhales slowly, like she's drawing on a cigarette. Her eyes are locked on mine, crushing me under her gaze. "Flattery is unbecoming."

"Facts," I correct, "are far from flattery, Miss Black."

She narrows her eyes to slits and sweeps her gaze over me. With a manicured nail she points to the scale. "Do it. Stop wasting time." Her last three words aren't sharp. I can tell she likes having her ego stroked, so I don't see it coming when she blindsides me.

I drop the dress and stand on the scale. She measures me, writes it down, and then sits on the edge of her desk without giving me permission to dress. So I stand there, scantily clad, staring at her polished, red, fuck-me heels.

Her voice is deep, direct, and laced with a warning tone. She balances the pen between her fore and middle fingers, moving it up and down. A fidgeting movement that isn't like her at all. I wait for her to speak and remain quiet, taking in the tension in her jaw and the way she tries to look relaxed, but she doesn't quite pull it off. I wouldn't have seen it when I first met her, but I do now. She's worried.

"I have a problem, Avery. A very serious dilemma. How am I to know, to be entirely confident you'll do whatever I ask without question tonight? In the past, you've proven reckless, and with this client, you can't be. You have to obey me completely without any insight, without any reason. I don't think you're capable of it. Your figure, yes, it's perfect. He prefers a woman with wider hips, even in an advisory role. But your discipline is utterly lacking."

I don't argue with her. I feel the entire plan shifting out of my hands, heading toward a free-fall. It has to be now, tonight. Everything is in place. For a moment, I think she knows we were in her house. Maybe Connie told her. Maybe she noticed the missing letter opener. Damn it.

In the past, my thoughts would have played across my face like a movie, but not tonight. I stand there, shoulders squared, relaxed but confident. A thought crosses my mind. It's slightly insane but I noticed it before, and it's impossible to ignore now. The way Black's eyes linger on my hips and the swell of my breasts. They remain there too long. Her lips part and she blinks slowly, thinking about something she can't have—something she wants to do but knows she shouldn't.

I act. She has to believe it's sincere, or it won't work. I'm not this woman. I don't feel this way—but I know she does. I step toward her in my heels and inhale slowly, letting the air make my chest rise. My breasts strain against the sheer lace, filling the bra. I come within a whisper of Black's face, close enough to kiss her, but not touching. I move my lips slowly, careful to barely brush the side of her mouth when I speak.

"Perhaps you never realized where my loyalties truly reside." I pull back slightly, enough for her to catch my eye. When our gazes lock, my pulse roars in my ears.

Her gaze drops to my lips, then my bra, and back to my mouth. "Loyalty is rare."

"I'm aware."

Black eyes me cautiously, but she doesn't pull away. "What are you suggesting?"

"Nothing that you don't already want." The words drip off my lips, slowly, surely.

Black is enthralled, watching me closely, breathing so hard that her chest swells making her tits brush mine for a moment before she exhales. Black lingers, fighting it. She knows I'm dead, gone after tonight. I suspected she wanted me, but I had no idea how much. Standing this close this long is tormenting her, but Black can't seem to pull herself back together. I rattled the woman with the heart of stone.

I risk lifting my hand and picking up a strand of her dark hair, letting it fall in a soft curl by her eyes. I sweep it back softly, barely touching her skin and she shudders. I finally get her. I understand her. Sex is power, but she has no interest in men. Not now. Her interest in Sean was never about him—it was me. She wanted me for herself. This changes things. I can use this. It might save us.

I chance it. I have to. There are too many lives on the line, and not just my own. I lean in, and close the distance between us, brushing my lips against hers. She stops breathing, freezes. The pen falls from her fingers and rolls under her desk. I lower my lashes and focus on her lips, pretending she's Sean. I think about how excited it makes him to have me so close, and then I forget myself for a moment. Eyes closed, I lean in and press my lips fully to hers, stroking her seam with my tongue. Black shudders and gasps before crumbling. Her hand finds my cheek, and I force myself to make that hand Sean's. I pretend she's him, lean into her palm and kiss her deeper. She purrs into my mouth and tangles her nails in my hair as she stands and presses her body to mine.

A voice and the rap, rap, rap of knuckles on the open door sound from behind me. "Is this a new job requirement?" Mel asks, half joking.

Trembling, Black pulls away quickly. Her eyes flash with a softness I've never seen on her. I'm not the one who breaks the kiss. I'm not the one who pulls away. She does and practically skitters behind her desk like a spooked cat. Mel caught her so off-guard that Black can't seem to speak, so I do.

"Yeah, come here." I hold out my arms to her and grin.

Mel snorts and waves a hand at me. "If it's all the same to you, I prefer men."

I shrug my shoulders and lie, "That's what I thought until rather recently." I turn and look at Black over my shoulder with a serene confidence I sure as hell don't feel. My mind was going nuts, and my body was fucking confused. Add in a baby lotion commercial, and I'll act completely insane in every possible way all at once.

Mel gives me a WTF look when Black has her eyes on the floor. I shrug like it's not a big deal and then give her a look that says to drop it. "Switching teams?" There's a dual meaning to her question, a sharpness about it that worries me.

Black gains control of herself again. Her head snaps up, and she scolds Mel. "Choosing sides isn't necessarily a switch, not when she's had no choice in the matter. I apologize for overlooking that aspect of things. It won't happen again."

Mel's jaw drops, and I smile. "Don't apologize. Ever. You're better than that. Better than all of us."

Mel's eyes widen as her forehead wrinkles, but Black doesn't see it. Her eyes are on me, locked with mine. I either just made the best decision or the worst one possible. It's still too soon to tell.

Black watches me, her eyes soft and her expression unreadable. I have no idea what she's thinking, but when she snaps out of it and glances at Mel, she's back to her old self. "Ladies, tonight's client has unusual tastes. I'm glad to see you're willing to go the extra mile, Miss Stanz."

The way she looks at me makes my cheeks burn. I don't hide my face. I just nod. It doesn't escape my notice that she uses my last name. She favors formality with those she respects. This set me apart from Mel in her mind. I'm not sure if that's a good thing, but at least now I know what frazzles her. It might help me gain the upper hand if I lose it tonight. I'll do anything, try anything to get through this. I don't like the thought of Black ending up in a body bag, but it's a necessary evil. Zipped, lifeless, and behind a layer of plastic is the only way I'll be free from her.

Something in the back of my mind cries out, forcing a tremor down my arms. My skin prickles in unison, from fingertips to neck, in a quick wave. It takes everything I have to keep the emotions off my face, to remain stoic—strong. But I feel it all the same. The blood on my hands, the man I shot—the man that rests in the woods. His location is unknown. His family never saw him again. He vanished without a trace, and I was the one responsible. I know it was self-defense, but that doesn't do a thing for my conscience. I could have and should have tried to find another way. The man would have lived. I could have survived. Killing is never justified, and yet, here I am preparing to slaughter the people trying to kill me. It's a preemptive move. It's justified. But part of me knows it's not. The part of me that's shoved into my mental closet, locked away forever, banished from the light of day because I can't face those facts, cries out in anguish. I don't like who I've become. It's too late to change course. If I do, my friends die with me.

Black blinks at me, waiting for a response to a question that I didn't hear. Mel widens her eyes and pulls her brows together giving me an 'answer her, you idiot' face.

At some point, the skeletons in my closet turned into demons. They aren't lifeless, waiting to be discovered. They're brewing just below the surface, always there, eager for a chance to ruin me. I'm not a fool. I know sifting through the things I've done will only make me crumble. If I have to be a fucking sociopath to live through tonight, I will be—I'll do it. I won't think twice. I'll slaughter myself to make sure my baby has a chance to live. I'll destroy any chance I have at reconciling who I am with what I've done if it means Sean will be able to hold his daughter. I wonder if this is how Constance ended up the way she is, if she got too close to the edge of the slippery slope and once fallen, couldn't rise. The race to the bottom isn't glorious. It isn't noble. It's despicable, and I'm part of it. I'm no better than Constance. No better than Black. I swallow hard as these thoughts flicker through my mind. They come in a rapid burst that barely consumes the time it takes to exhale.

I hedge, as I try to stop the tidal wave of horror building within me. "I'm not certain I understood that. Can you say it another way?"

Mel sighs so loud that she spits. She talks with her hands, annoyed. "Miss Black wants us to stay together tonight. She's making an introduction that has connections to people you'll want as clients when you're a madam." Mel knows I wasn't listening and repeats the facts, so I don't miss anything. "Black set up the introduction, and already presented him the terms. All you have to do is show up with his spec sheet and walk him through filling it out. Oh, and she's coming with us." Mel flicks a finger toward Black and gives me a hopeless look.

Black wasn't supposed to be there. That's not part of the plan and causes a major problem for the rest of us. "I'm sorry, you're coming?" I look at Miss Black and smile at her softly, lowering my voice to a gentle whisper. "That's not really necessary, is it?" I touch her arm with the pads of my fingers and barely brush her skin.

Black becomes rigid, stopping mid-breath, with her lungs filling her chest. It forces her breasts to swell and push against the red fabric of her dress. Her dark eyes meet mine, and she lets out the breath slowly. "No, it's not. In fact, I hadn't planned on escorting you. However..." her voice trails off as her gaze remains locked on mine with an unreadable expression. Is that regret? I can't tell.

Mel offers, "I can handle him if needed. Plus Gabe will be around, so you only need to come out if you want."

"And I want to." There's a finality in her tone that closes the conversation.

I glance at Mel, and know we're both thinking the same thing. We're screwed.

CHAPTER 17

We were supposed to confer with Gabe on the drive to Vic Jr.'s estate, finalize any last-second changes with Marty, and then rendezvous with Sean and Henry once we were inside the building. That's not possible with Black in tow.

I sit at the back of the limo and trade nervous glances with Mel. Neither of us says a word as we speed toward the South Shore of Long Island. Gabe doesn't look at us, doesn't have any telltale signs of tension from the front seat. I wonder how long he's been undercover because I'm ready to puke.

I twist the gold bracelet around my wrist and rub the round black bead between my fingers. Mel's matches mine perfectly, but she doesn't fidget. The movement draws Black's eye, and she glances at my fingers, the stone, and then up at my face.

"You got the bracelet fitted, I see."

What? I glance at the golden band. It's identical to my old one with one exception—it's the right size. I forgot my original bracelet was so big I had to wear it on my ankle. Black notices little details like that, details Henry overlooked when making the bracelets.

I smile like it's a fond memory and drop the bead. "Yes, it fits much better now. Doesn't fall off."

Black inclines her head, holds out a hand, and waits for me to offer my wrist. Mel carefully ignores us. If the bracelets don't make it into Vic's estate, then we're all fucked. My heart pounds as I offer my wrist to the woman. She takes my hand and examines the fit, nodding and then releasing my arm.

"Well done."

I swallow hard and say nothing. Her gaze resumes the blank stare forward. The car fills with a palpable tension the closer we get to Vic's. When we arrive, we pull into the winding, tree-lined driveway and head toward the great house. It's set back on the property, offering the seclusion and privacy a sick bastard like Vic needs.

My heart slams into my ribs, and my palms grow slick with sweat. I focus on the mission, trying to remain calm. If I lose my shit, I won't be able to think. And it's evident I'll need to be on my toes tonight. The car pulls into the circle drive in front of the home. The façade is slate and gray stone. Lights flood across the stone, accenting the sweeping architectural lines of the building. Tall narrow trees form spires in the flowerbeds, and in the center of the circle drive is an enormous fountain big enough to swim in. It has four tiers where water trickles down into a massive base that looks more like an in-ground pool than landscaping embellishments.

Gabe stops the car and walks around, opens the door for Black. She glides out and straightens. Mel slips out next, leaving me alone in the car. Gabe offers me his hand, and as I clasp my palm in his, I feel the scrape of paper being pressed into my palm. I say nothing, and pretend to adjust my bra strap after standing. I turn briefly, adjust my bra, and stuff the piece of paper out of sight. I can't read it now. She'll see.

Gabe notices but says nothing as he climbs back into the driver's seat and pulls away. My stomach fills with lead, and I can't seem to make my feet move. Death waits for me in that house. I can't go.

Black moves in long, lean strides toward the enormous front door. Mel is behind her until she realizes I'm not moving. I can barely breathe. It feels like an elephant sat on my chest.

Mel hooks her arm through mine and leans in, whispering, "You can do this."

I say nothing. Instead, I stare at the door and feel my stomach sink into my heels. "This isn't right."

"No shit, but there aren't many options right now. We can't abort. She'll know we know. Fuck, Vic will know and he'll be coming for us. This is our only chance. Move your feet. Stop thinking. Just act."

I nod a tiny bit and glance over at her. "Is that what you do?"

"Yeah, there's a reason why I practice with knives, Avery. Muscle memory is faster than anything else. Don't think. Just act."

Black is at the door, looks back at us slowly walking toward her, and rings the bell.

I whisper, "Okay. Once Marty is here, everything will be fine. He'll get the bracelet to the security room, and Sean will come for me."

"Right. Marty already has everything worked out. When we see him, the hardest part of this shit will be over. The rest is up to Marty, Sean, and Henry. Then you and I get the fuck out."

I nod and glance over at her. "In case we don't make it—"

Mel cuts me off, "We'll make it. It'll be fine, so there's no need for any sentiment right now. Focus. We have to stall Black and Vic long enough for Marty to get Sean and Henry inside. We can do that."

"Black can throw the whole thing off."

Mel glares at Black. "I know."

"Well, then what?"

"We wing it and fight like hell." Before we're within earshot of Black, Mel releases my arm, pretends to be adjusting my dress, tugs at the skirt, and smooths the bodice. "And remember, surviving justifies anything. Don't think. Just act."

I turn toward the front door and feel an icy finger work its way up my spine as the mammoth door is opens, and light pours onto the doorstep. Miss Black's slick voice fills my head, "Miss Black here to see Victor. I have an appointment."

CHAPTER 18

We're led down hallways by a man I've never seen before. I glance around for Marty, not seeing him. Panic tries to claw its way up from my gut and into my throat, but I slam it back down. It doesn't mean anything. As we walk through the house, Mel and I follow Black in silence. The butler—dude in a posh black suit—opens a door to a room with massive windows on one end, thick grooved, floor-to-ceiling wood paneling and ornately carved moldings.

He ushers us inside. "Mr. Campone will be with you shortly. Please make yourself comfortable." The man retreats, closing the doors behind him.

This isn't right. Marty should have met us en route. That was the plan. I glance at Mel who seems totally calm. She walks over to the windows and looks out onto the sprawling lawn. Massive floodlights illuminate sections of the yard, accentuating an Olympic-sized swimming pool, casitas, and a tennis court. Trees form a wall of dark shadows at the back edge of the property.

Miss Black saunters across the room to an old desk and sits in the high-backed leather chair behind it. She settles in and steeples her fingers as if she owns the place.

I want to pace, but can't. I chance a glance at Black and catch her eyes. I feel my lips tip up into a nervous smile. She looks away from me, her eyes cutting to the side swiftly. The butterflies in my stomach turn to stone and plop down one by one until I'm so nauseated I'm ready to puke. I walk over to a section of built-in bookcases and pull a thick old book from the shelf. I open it and pretend to read, carefully pulling Gabe's note and placing it in the center of the page. There are two words scribbled hastily. Eight little letters that pierce through me, ripping me apart:

SHE KNOWS

I feel my back stiffen as I close the book with the note still inside and slide it back onto the shelf. Before I can say anything to Mel, the doors open and Vic walks in with two men in his wake.

Vic is dressed in black, hip-hugging slacks and has a freshly shaven head. His eyes are hard and lifeless, which appears even more unsettling when combined with the playful smile on his lips. An icy pang of panic rushes through my veins when he looks my way. He opens his arms with a smile as if he were going to hug me. "Sis! Good to see you again. You ran off so fast last time we didn't get to talk business."

I force myself to calmly spit out his name. "Victor."

Mel eyes the man wearily and scans his minions. It's three on three, assuming Black is on our side. I can tell she's wondering the same thing. The longer we go without spotting Marty, the worse I feel. It means nothing went right, and we're already dead.

Vic turns toward Miss Black and laughs bitterly. "I don't recall you being invited here tonight."

Her steepled fingers fold together, and she looks up at him, completely calm. "Delighted to see you, too, Victor. There's a matter we need to address prior to any further discussion this evening."

Victor doesn't hide his temper. "Are you fucking me over? You know what I do to people who are two-bit liars, don't you, Black? I know you do, so what's so fucking important you'd risk pissing me off?"

Black stands, walks directly toward me and loops her fingers around my bracelet. She yanks and the clasp pops, breaking the gold chain free. "This isn't mine. You might want to look into it before the evening advances. I'd hate to see you spend good money on something that won't come to fruition." She dangles the gold bracelet over his palm before dropping it.

Vic lifts it, looks at the stone. "Ladies, care to share what you've got here?" The response is demanded. His voice lacks the questioning tone. Vic's eyes drift to Mel's wrist, and, when he spots the matching bracelet, he snaps his fingers and jerks his head toward her. "Take it."

His men walk over to Mel and rip the bracelet from her wrist. Mel doesn't fight back, doesn't react. Everything is going to hell when the door flies open and Marty storms in. He's dressed in black fatigues with a gun strapped to his hip. There's a wire that connects to a walkie-talkie in his back hip pocket. Four men flank him, and it's clear he's in charge, which surprises me. I thought Marty blended here.

Marty's voice sounds hard, firm. "Sorry to interrupt but it's necessary." He stands at attention like a solider reporting for duty.

Hope fills my chest as Marty's gaze lands on me. Everything will be all right now. I can finally breathe, and certainty squares my shoulders and lifts my chin. He'll get Sean to me. He knows my backup plan too. I can do it. He can help me. I can do this, and it will all work out. Thank God. I've never been so happy to see anyone in my entire life.

Vic dangles the two bracelets in the air and asks the men, "Do you know what these are?"

Marty steps forward to pluck the jewelry from Vic's hands. "Yes, sir. This is the device I described. It's housed in the bead."

Mel realizes it before I do. As my heart sinks and denial cries out within me, she screams, "You fucking bastard!"

Mel continues to spew nasty curses at him as a guard lunges at her, attempting to restrain her. She slashes at him when he tries to pin her arm behind her back. A primal scream tears from her throat as she whirls around, knives in hand, slashing at anyone who comes near her. Two more men come forward, and the three of them force her to the floor before she can inflict any serious damage. They took her down without any effort at all. She's dragged from the room, promising Marty a painful death. Her voice disappears down the hallway, and then suddenly falls silent.

"Marty," I say, my voice quavering. Heart pounding I stare at him and feel my jaw tightening. "I thought you cared."

Vic watches with delight. Black is unexpressive as usual, still behind the desk like it's just another day at the office.

Marty's voice is cold. "You thought wrong."

Eyes narrowed to thin slits I scream at him, "How could you do this? After everything we went through. Why didn't you kill me before? Why fucking wait 'til now? Why pretend to be my friend?"

Marty glances to the side at Vic. Vic grins and gestures happily, "Go ahead and tell her. It's a marvelous story, this one. So much potential. It's nice to see what you're made of, Masterson."

Marty steps toward me and gazes down, his golden eyes hard. "Vic hired me. That part was true—all of it—but there was a tiny omission, and it's the only reason you're still alive."

My jaw slowly drops as I put the pieces together. Marty saved me even though Vic Senior wanted me dead. Why? Why risk it?

Black speaks up, sounding bored, "Victor— his father—hired Marty, but his loyalty has always been elsewhere, even before Victor the elder was gunned down. You're alive because Vic Jr. wanted it that way. Marty is a mercenary, Avery. He works for your brother."

I mouth the word NO, but no sound comes out.

Marty remains still and says nothing. He's not smug, arrogant, or anything. He stares straight ahead like a soldier, while Vic Jr. slow-claps, laughing at me.

"The look on your face is fucking beautiful. I can't wait to see what comes next." He pauses, lifts a finger, and adds, "Wait for it."

The crack of a gunshot shatters the night.

He turns his head toward Marty, asks, "Was that it?"

Marty shakes his head. "One more."

A second shot rings out before I realize what it means. Vic grins. "You don't do warning shots, do you, Masterson?"

"No, sir."

My chest feels like it's ripping in two. I run toward the window and look out. Two bodies float facedown in the pool with ribbons of red flowing from their black clothing, tinting the sparkling water. I can make out the long lines of the trench coats from here. The belts float to the surface of the pool as the waves from the initial splash calm.

A walkie-talkie on Marty's hip makes a static sound as someone talks into his earpiece. Marty nods at Vic Jr. "It's done."

"Finally! Two Ferros down. I always start with the hardest to kill. It makes the rest of the game so much easier." He chortles a deranged fit of laughter and then walks over to me, slaps his hand on my shoulder. I try to slink away from him, from his touch, but he doesn't let go. "Do you like to play games, Avery? Because I have a few picked out, just for you—and now there's no one to save you. Not Sean. Not Mel. And, sure as hell, not Marty. No one." He wraps his lips around the last two words and smiles sadistically in my face.

Terror courses through my veins, but I can't move. I can't speak. My hand is on my stomach as horror hits me hard.

Vic steps closer and whispers in my ear, "It's just you and me, little sister.

CHAPTER 19

~HOLLY~

Bet you never thought you'd see my name as a chapter heading, huh? It's a little weird, and this is the only time I've ever put myself into a book like this, but there's something you need to know. It's something super important—something you might have missed if I didn't put it right here.

THIS SERIES WILL CONCLUDE WITH VOLUME 23.

Thank you for embracing something new—the concept of a fan-driven series. That alone was a can of worms. You may have heard by now that *The Arrangement* series was originally planned to be four volumes, but fans loved it so much I presented the option to continue and asked the fans to vote on it. Readers decided if there would be more books, and what would happen at certain points in the story. One of the biggest, most complicated decisions was Mel's and Avery's friendship. The story follows the paths you selected. It was like having a storyteller right there telling you the tale. That is the reason we are at twenty-two volumes.

Few authors would willingly undertake an open-ended story and allow fans to steer the weaving of the tale. It creates plot issues of iceberg proportions and requires a ton more work. I'm a little nuts, and think challenges are fun. I enjoy reading your comments and thoughts. I've loved letting you guys vote to determine which direction the story should go. Your answers surprised me at times, but made writing the story a more intense experience— which was an unexpected thrill.

The Arrangement series was an experiment from concept to completion, and I loved every second of it. Prior to *The Arrangement, Volume 1*, I'd just completed the *Demon Kissed* series. In it was a character (Eric) who started as a good man, but by the end of the series had fallen. Eric was my inspiration for Sean Ferro. He made me want to examine in a contemporary setting the life of someone who was despised—a soul that had fallen down the edge of the slippery slope with no hope of escape.

When we meet him, Sean is at the bottom of the pit. His mother, Constance, is as deep as you can get in that soul-sucking chasm. Mel is clinging to the rim by her fingernails, refusing to fall. Meanwhile, Avery wants to pitch herself over the edge and sled to the bottom. She's in so much pain she can't take it anymore. But Sean intervenes, and she gets so focused on pulling him out that she forgets about herself.

At the core of this tale, is a question—can a bad person be redeemed? Can a soul heal enough to both feel compassion and act on it after being torn apart? How would that happen? What would prompt a change of that magnitude?

Writing this series has been an amazing experience. So many of you, from all walks of life, have contacted me and described how stories like this help to heal a broken soul. I've been touched by the response to this story, by the emotional reactions it evokes. We are all struggling and life is filled with so much suffering. Tales provide an escape from this harsh reality, a way to express the feelings and emotions we haven't yet found the words to explain. They offer a way out of the pit even when there is no Sean to save us.

Thank you for encouraging me to write this tale, for helping me explore the complexity of Sean & Avery's life. Without you, I wouldn't have spun this narrative. Without you, this series wouldn't be this close to production (more info on that to come). You are the reason I love this job, why I continue to do what I do. You make a difference and this series is an awesome testimony to what we can do together.

The Arrangement 23 will be the final volume in *The Arrangement* series. It concludes the backstory of Sean and Avery. The other Ferro world books released to date also tell the backstories of individual characters (Peter in *Damaged*, Bryan in *The Proposition*, Jon in *Stripped*, Nick in *The Wedding Contract*, Jos in *Easy*, Trystan in *Broken Promises*, etc.) When these individual stories conclude later this year, we will transition into one narrative with all the remaining Ferros in one series.

Many people are asking me if I'll ever create another fan-driven series. While there are no plans at this point, I'll be certain to let you know when I'm ready to accept the challenge again. Crafting this tale has been an amazing experience.

The Arrangement 23 is available for pre-order now. The release date is set for March 2017, although there's the possibility it may be released before that. Keep an eye out. With the conclusion of this series, there will also be a lot of prizes and fun on Facebook. Be sure to join us and visit the page often for the latest updates.

You guys are amazing! Thank you so much for sharing this journey with me!

COMING SOON:

THE ARRANGEMENT 23

The conclusion to H.M. Ward's *New York Times*
& USA Today Bestselling Arrangement Series

PRE-ORDER IT TODAY!

***

Make sure you don't miss it!
Text HMWARD (one word) to 24587
to receive a text reminder on release day.

READY FOR MORE?
PRE-ORDER THESE TITLES TODAY!

~A DAMAGED WEDDING~ (September 20)
~HOT GUY~ (November 15)
~EASY~ (December 27)
~EASY 2~ (January 10)
~EASY 3~ (January 31)
~EASY 4~ (February 14)
~EASY 5~ (February 28)
~THE ARRANGEMENT 23~ (March 28)

*****

NEED A BOOK FOR YOUR KID?

~RISE OF THE OLYMPIANS~ (FREE)
~RISE OF THE OLYMPIANS 2~
~RISE OF THE OLYMPIANS 3~
~RISE OF THE OLYMPIANS 4~
~RISE OF THE OLYMPIANS 5~
~RISE OF THE OLYMPIANS 6~

MORE FERRO FAMILY BOOKS

JONATHAN FERRO
~STRIPPED~
******

TRYSTAN SCOTT
~BROKEN PROMISES~
******

NICK FERRO
~THE WEDDING CONTRACT~
*****

BRYAN FERRO
~THE PROPOSITION~
*****

SEAN FERRO
~THE ARRANGEMENT~
******

PETER FERRO GRANZ
~DAMAGED~
******

MORE ROMANCE BY H.M. WARD

SCANDALOUS

SCANDALOUS 2

SECRETS

THE SECRET LIFE OF TRYSTAN SCOTT

DEMON KISSED

CHRISTMAS KISSES

OVER YOU

HOT GUY

And more.

To see a full book list, please visit:
www.hmward.com/pages/books.html

CAN'T WAIT FOR *H.M. WARD'S NEXT STEAMY BOOK?*

Let her know by leaving stars and telling her
what you liked about
THE ARRANGEMENT 22
in a review!

ABOUT THE AUTHOR
H.M. WARD

New York Times bestselling author HM Ward
continues to reign as the queen of independent
publishing. She is swiftly approaching 13 MILLION
copies sold, placing her among the literary titans.
Articles pertaining to Ward's success have appeared in
The New York Times, USA Today, and Forbes to name
a few. This native New Yorker resides in Texas with her
family, where she enjoys working on her next book.

You can interact with this bestselling author at:
Twitter: @HMWard
Facebook: AuthorHMWard
Webpage: www.hmward.com

4203

Made in the USA
San Bernardino, CA
16 September 2016